SCIS.
KILLER

LEGS OF DEATH

MATT SQUEEZER

ISBN: 9798831278699

Order more books and videos at WrestleMen.com.

Chapter One

His glazed-over eyes looked helplessly into mine as small red dots formed on his contorted face. His hands firmly grasped the sides of my sinewy thighs but were unable to pry them from around his slender neck. Strands of drool seeped from the corners of his lips. He moaned a pleasing moan, as if this is how he had always wanted to die: trapped within the sweaty crotch of a virile man. I held him there for over an hour, taunting him again and again before applying the final death squeeze. Another drug dealer off the streets.

As I always do, I snapped pictures of his final throes, when his panic was at its peak. Something about seeing my thick legs around another man's neck excites me, especially when my victims give in to my control. My legs coiled around him like the thickest part of an anaconda. They'd grown stronger and bigger over the years, no doubt due to these weekly workouts as I slither in and out of dark and destitute places across the country. Places where drug dealers, thieves, and murderers hide. Like in run-down trailers and abandoned houses up long gravel drives hidden from the main roads. Or in the dirty alleyways of the inner cities. But often times, in the best suites of expensive hotels. Money-hungry men doing bad deeds are easy prey.

This one I found in the back swamps of Louisiana. I tracked him down from security-camera footage on the local news. Jett was his name, wanted for supplying ten grams of cocaine to a bunch of college students, two of which died within the past week, and five others still in the ICU. It was a dirty coke, contaminated with traces of fentanyl. The horrific details of how the two kids died—choking on their own vomit while experiencing seizure-like spasms—were recounted by their grieving classmates. Choked out, I thought. With body-contorting spasms. The punishment would have to match the crime.

I was in my van, a 2002 Dodge Ram that I had converted into a traveling home. Many of my victims would meet their fate within these metal walls. It made transporting and disposing of their bodies much more convenient. Luring them inside was the key, but I had my special ways of doing so. Seeing as drug dealers like to keep their transactions under wraps, it was easy to get them to comply.

I recognized Jett's neck tattoo, a poorly designed scorpion, when he stopped at the Wawa across the street from where I had parked tonight. It was only a few hours after I watched the news footage from my phone. So I slowly pulled my van up to a pump while he was inside the store. When he came out of the door with a small sub and a large beer, I made my move.

I asked if he could tell me how many miles it was to Baton Rouge. Told him I was going to a party the next day, where I'd meet up with a group of old wrestling buddies from my team back in Iowa. There was a UFC-type fight in town, and we were going to make it "one hell of a good night."

Funny how it is, that mentioning wrestling to another man easily grabs his attention. It's both the curiosity and the lure of male bodies physically connecting and releasing pent-up aggression that does it. And, no doubt, the homoeroticism of it all. I would use this to my advantage this night.

I knew Jett was on the run, and coming with me to ride in my van was an easy way to leave behind his own vehicle and evade police. But I'd have to be careful. I wanted to avoid detection too. And I didn't want to lead on that I knew what he had done. So I told him instead to meet me a few miles up. There, off to the side and hard to detect without street lights, was a narrow dirt path that ran along the edge of a secluded swamp. We could park and have a few beers, and I could teach him those holds he had always wanted to try. He had mentioned the rear naked choke and a few others in our brief moments by the pumps.

Within minutes both our cars were hidden from sight. As we drank our beers and listened to the mating frogs on this humid summer night, I slowly seduced him into my van where he met his ending. In the early morning hours, I opened the back doors and pulled his lifeless body into the swamp, the water above my knees before I let go. Then I put his car in neutral and pushed it in after him. The toxicology reports would reveal his inebriated state, and it would appear he had driven off the road. The crushed trachea, neck bruises, and blood-shot eyes would be my marks, marks they wouldn't be able to explain at first. Not until, perhaps, it happened again and again in a familiar pattern state after state. I would soon be known as the SCISSOR KILLER.

I've always had an insatiable need to lock my legs around someone, ever since I was a kid. Even well before puberty. In grade school PE class, I would sneak up on other boys as we sat on the floor waiting for our gym teacher to arrive. I'd snatch their bodies between my thighs like some sort of Venus Flytrap or octopus monster. They didn't stand a chance once I locked my ankles in a straight or figure-four scissor. Boys would place bets on who could escape first. I'd tell them they'd have to give me their lunch money if they couldn't break free within two minutes. A lot of boys went hungry those years. Still, it never seemed to stop them from trying. They'd struggle and struggle, and it would only make me want to hold them even longer, and tighter. "The more you move, the more I squeeze," I'd tell them.

In high school, coach asked me to join the wrestling team. I had great stamina, and I used the reverse scissor very effectively to pin a guy's shoulders to the mat. Photos they'd print the next day of their faces lodged in my crotch and butt turned me on. I'd seek out similar photos in wrestling books at the school library. Occasionally, I'd find a good scissor hold image in the encyclopedia. I'd tear them out when no one was looking, and slip them into a book by my bed.

I wrestled all through college, and even became division champ in my senior year. Once school was over, I was left with an inescapable void. I needed to continue to use my powerful legs, and with my degree in criminal justice, I sought out ways to bring both together.

I took up submission wrestling at a local dojo near Detroit. Got a lot of guys in triangle chokes back then. They'd always ask me to demonstrate any leg holds. Couple of times the sensei and I rolled around in private. Doug knew what he wanted from me, and I never let him down. I'd knock him out every time after hours of full-on sweating. Couldn't wait to toss his arm out of the way and make him suffer with his face pressed deep into my bulge as I worked my calves behind his head. He said that was a dirty move, but it never stopped him from asking me to stick around after class every Friday night.

When I got a job with a local police station, I spent all my spare hours in the gym pumping up my thighs and calves with all the machines. Couple of times I asked some of the smaller guys if I could lift them with my legs while doing ab crunches. I'd hoist myself up with my forearms on the resting pads, lock my thighs and calves around their torsos, and pull them off the ground. Sometimes I'd give them a tight squeeze while they dangled there. They'd gasp a bit every time I raised up. With each ab crunch I'd tighten a little more. There was no shortage of guys who wanted to help me out. One time I locked two guys in at once.

That was about five years ago, when I decided to go out on my own. I got tired of examining cold cases, where investigators gave up on finding those who perpetrated crimes around the city. Drugs were rampant, and dealers seemed to be on every street corner. And then there were the rapists who some-how escaped prosecution because they had good lawyers, or were never tested for their DNA. Repeat offenders of theft and grand larceny were out on the street and on probation within a year, in many cases. And then there were the unsolved murders. It seemed that the justice system just wasn't working as it should. Too many victims, and not enough punishment, I thought. I was going to change that.

Jose Sanchez escaped a twenty-year sentence for forced entry, robbery, and assault. His victim was a 64-year-old grandmother on Newberry Street. She was just returning from a neighbor's house after a dinner celebration. Before she could lock the door behind her, Jose sprang out from the side bushes and shoved her inside. With the door closed, he proceeded to tie her hands to the bottom stair-rail post with heavy-duty twine he found in her back-yard garden. Then he ransacked the house, search-ing for jewelry, priceless heirlooms, and straight-up cash. In between rooms, he would threaten to kill her with the twine. He told her he'd use it to severe her head off if she wouldn't comply with his de-mands. He wanted access to a small safe box he found in a hallway closet. Fearing for her life, Anne Bloomfield told him to check the half-circle drawer table by the front door, where a small planter rested on top of a delicate doily. Next to it was a framed picture of her and her deceased husband, Stan Bloomfield. He had died of Covid a few months prior.

Jose snatched the box, grabbed a set of keys, and slipped out the back door when he heard sirens approaching. A neighbor, Martha Wilcox, had heard the commotion inside while returning a dinner pan and contacted police. Because Jose was wearing a mask, neither of the two women could get a good look at him.

Investigators thought they had their man when Jose was caught five miles away at a pawn shop with an old diamond ring the next day. But Anne's memory was fading, and she couldn't remember if it was one of hers or not. And Jose left no obtainable DNA in the house, so he escaped prosecution. I was tipped off by an underground informant that Jose had confessed to the crime, and similar others. I would track him to a run-down St. Louis neighborhood.

Chapter 2

Moments after entering the Peabody-Darst-Webbe neighborhood from I-55, I was hot on Jose's trail. My informant told me to check the local liquor stores late at night. Jose grew up in the area and was known to stop for a bottle of whiskey at Ray's Liquor after each robbery. A sort of celebration. His targets were always Detroit and Chicago, never his home turf. He'd do this about once a month, then lay low.

I parked my van across from the liquor store for the first three nights, scoping out the place for signs of his whereabouts. On the third night, just as I was about to pull away, Jose showed up as planned. I drove slowly along Tucker Street as he walked down the cracked sidewalk a few blocks before turning left at Elmhurst. He was swinging a bottle in a crumbled paper bag and could barely keep himself upright. Chances are he had been celebrating for days. Drunk prey is my favorite. Makes for an easy kill. But I wanted to spend some time with this one.

He entered a small, shabby house at 201 Elmhurst, and I parked my van not far away. I was able to see with binoculars that he didn't live alone. I could detect another man with him, guy about the same gangly size with a full-on neck tattoo of a spi-der web or something. They both seemed to be drinking that first night, well past 2 a.m. I pulled away before sunrise and spent the first day figuring out how I wanted to take him. My legs were getting restless and they needed a good feeding soon.

For four days I stalked Jose, watching his every move outside of his house. He spent a bit of time mucking around with weights at Darius Gym on Belmont. His build reminded me of the smaller guys that I'd use as props in my ab workouts. At night, he'd stagger out of bars and liquor stores like a drunk pink panther. His jeans sank below his waist, revealing his skinny waist. It couldn't be much more than 29 inches, the size of each of my quads. Every time I saw him turn down the dimly lit alleyway shortcut to his house, I felt a rise in my crotch. It is how I concocted my plan.

On Friday, I entered the gym and worked up a sweat on the leg press. It was 6 p.m., about the time that Jose would show up. And he did, right on cue. I wanted to observe my prey up close, like a snake in the grass. I wanted to analyze every part of his body, every one of his movements, and all his weaknesses. Seemed he only worked out to pass time before drinking. To make appearances. To probably sell drugs.

He looked over a few times while I squatted 250 on the half rack. His cocky look, one that I'd seen many times before on immoral men that could never set themselves straight, fueled my passion to snuff him out. Somehow, along with my workout, this energized me more.

It was 8 p.m. and another round of men showed up. A tougher crowd, the kind that stayed away from nighttime crowds at dive bars and restaurants. Men with full-chest tattoos and smiles as dark as the iron in their hands. Men with legs as big as mine, but without the desire to use them. Such a waste. If I could, I would train an army of them to kill by thigh and calf. Trap, wrap, and squeeze the crap out of others. But I was on a mission, and I couldn't get caught up in that now. I needed to focus on the meal at hand, and tonight's main course was crushed Sanchez.

I hit up the showers at 9 p.m., and Jose entered as I was toweling off. No doubt he wanted to see me naked, as he didn't seem like the type that bathed much. He nodded one of those guy nods, the kind that acknowledges an appreciation of another man. I nodded back while flexing and drying my calf muscles. Gave him a good taste of his future fate.

About twenty minutes later, I slipped out the front and passed by Jose, who was talking smack to his seedy boys about getting some booze and making it a wild night: Rumple Minze, whiskey, beer, and whatever they could grab down the street. He was too busy to notice me entering my van and pulling away from the curb. But I would be ready for him when the moon rose high tonight.

The sounds of group chatter by Ray's liquor store faded into the staggered steps of one man as Jose parted with his gang of losers and headed back home. It was a little after 2:30 a.m., and I had already left the van and placed myself strategically in his path. The alleyway by the liquor store was as dark as my black compression shorts, which is all I had on from the gym. They were ripe with my smell. My sweaty, shirtless torso reflected glints of moonlight as I climbed the metal fire escape anchored into the side of the brick building. I rested on the first landing like a python in waiting.

It's that moment before the kill that takes me to places in my head that I cannot explain. It arouses me. My cock, fully engorged with blood, pulsated with anticipation. The more it bulged, the more I could feel the pressure of the nylon fabric that held it tight against my body. I stretched out my legs, crossed my ankles, and pumped my thighs up and down to get the muscles ready. Then I kicked off my shoes. Tonight would be a barefoot take. I like the raw feeling of my feet and legs fully exposed. It's animalistic. Tribal.

Jose turned the corner and shuffled down the alley a few steps before resting against the wall. He lifted a paper bag he held at his side and took a swig of the contents. Then he laughed a small laugh, like he had just remembered a joke. Or the alcohol was finally taking him to the places he needed to go. As he lowered his one arm down, I could see him raise the other. He slid his hand down the front of his loose pants and started to fondle his crotch. I listened as he moaned a few times before he lifted the paper bag up to his lips again. He staggered farther down the alley, just feet away from me. From my higher vantage point, I could see him pull his zipper down. He repeated the moaning and groping. It was clear that he had done this before, gotten himself off in this alleyway. It *was* the perfect spot. Dark, secluded, and partially obstructed by large brown trash bins at both ends. I began to rub my bulge, too, as I prepared for my attack.

Jose pulled off his shirt and stuffed one end into his waistband. He rubbed his chest and grazed over his nipples before arching back to shoot his load. He shook several times, almost falling to the ground at one point before finishing himself off. Though he couldn't see me, it was as if he were drawn to move closer. That somehow, he knew. That the pheromones of another man in the vacinity were hypnotizing him. My pheromones. Luring him. Seducing him. With two steps more I made my move.

Holding tight to the runner along the edge of the first landing, I lowered my torso and lassoed my legs around his naked chest. It happened so fast he dropped his bottle and let out a sharp gasp. I bent my legs around him in a figure-four and pressed my thighs into his ribcage. My left calf muscle sank deep across his breastbone. My right foot weaved around his hipbone. When I had him fully locked in, I began my ab workout.

As with the small guys at the gym, I lifted Jose up over and over again. But this time, I used all the strength in my legs to compress his torso. At the top of each lift, I flexed my feet as if they were the ends of a rope, and flexing them pulled the rope tighter. I learned this technique after rolling with so many guys at the Detroit dojo. It's a mind and body thing: fitting your legs around another body and forcing them to encircle rather than just bend. I made sure there were no gaps between the skin of my legs and the skin of his bare chest.

Jose's body was like an extension of mine, and the tighter I squeezed the nicer it felt. My cock pressed hard into his back muscles with each lift. He grasped at my calves a few times, but there was no way he could pry himself free. Much of the air had already left his lungs when I first nabbed him, and my continuous tightening assured that little would reenter.

For close to three minutes I jacked him up and down like Tarzan trapping a thief in the jungle while dangling from a tree. I used to get off to those movie scenes, and I would rewind the tapes to watch them again and again. But this was no movie. This was real life. It was my life now. And it would be the death of Jose tonight.

With my thighs locked in place, I flexed in my hamstrings. They cut deep between his ribs to fill any void. Then, I sank in my death grip. One by one each of his ribs busted under the intense pressure. One must have shot deep into his lungs, as he gasped and tried to cry out. But you can't scream if you can't breathe. I let him hang between my crushing legs a few more minutes until his asphyxiation was complete.

Once Jose's limp, lifeless body hunched over my locked calves, I let go and dropped him to the dirty asphalt. I pulled myself up onto the landing and rubbed my bulge over and over again until I came too. I slid my hand inside my black trunks and felt the thick, wet jizz with my hand. Then I brought my hand to my face and rubbed a bit on my chest and thighs. Someday I would coat my prey with it, but I had to be careful not to leave evidence. At least, not this time.

I retrieved my shoes and snuck out the back of the alley. But I wanted more that night. And I knew where Jose lived. So I quickly returned to Jose's dead body and lifted the keys from his pocket. There was something deeply satisfying in his lifeless eyes. I knelt down and peered into them and cocked my head sideways. It was as if he had wanted me to take him all along, like this was his fantasy back at the gym when he entered the showers.

I pulled his cock out from his pants, stroked it a few times, and let his remaining jizz spill out onto the pavement.

Jose's roommate was my next target, and he would surely be asleep by now. I knew of no crime that he may have committed, but to me, he was a criminal by association. And when you're hungry, as I often am, you have to eat.

I made my way around the back of the property and peeked through all the windows. Entering a residence was always a risk. And I couldn't guarantee that there weren't others staying there. Like more hoodlums crashing for the night. But my instincts told me that these two were loners, hoarding all the catch to themselves. Now there would be just one left, and I knew how I wanted to take him.

Chapter 3

One of the basement windows was pushed open, and so I slid my body through and carefully stepped down to the floor. It was a damp, musty basement. Dark. Just the kind of place a creature of the night would like to hide and trap its prey.

I started to get aroused again when I spotted an old bundle of rope hanging from a wall hook. There wasn't much else in sight, except a dilapidated hot water tank and an old washer and dryer. The floor was covered with dirt and debris.

As I moved farther in, I noticed a plastic curtain blocking off a portion of the space. Behind it was no surprise, given the neighborhood. A small table and bench covered with beakers, test tubes, and a large glass bottle were the telltale signs of a make-shift meth lab. I'd seen them many times before while with the force. But this setup appeared un-used. Everything had a coating of dust. They proba-bly gave up and turned to old-fashioned crimes. Didn't want to put in the hard work to make quality sell. Or they were just too stupid to be chemists. Surprised the place hadn't blown up.

I exited the room and slowly made my way to the stairwell, making sure not to knock anything over. It was a narrow staircase, wooden, certain to creak if I wasn't careful. The steps had gaps in between that you could see through and behind. A metal chair was hidden underneath, along with a small table and ashtray. Seemed like an odd place to have a smoke. I sat down in the chair for a moment and concocted my plan.

Twenty minutes later I had everything set up. It was time to take action before daylight. Hiding under the stairwell, I pounded sharply on the ceiling rafters. Nothing. No reaction. I did it again, then two more times. Finally, I heard the sound of someone speaking above in a restless tone.

"Jose, man, you home?"

I pounded again on the rafters.

"Oh man, did you lock yourself out again? Stupid fool."

I waited and listened till I heard the door open at the top of the steps.

"You down there? You shitfaced I bet." He flipped a switch and a dim bulb came on in the center of the basement.

I was quiet as the thug took to each of the steps, the wood creaking beneath his bare feet. Halfway down, I made my move.

I thrust my hands between the fifth and sixth steps from the bottom and grabbed his ankles tight. Then I pulled back until he toppled over, his hands just able to stop his head from hitting the bottom step. He screamed out in shock.

"What the fuck!"

I wasted no time. I pulled his body back hard until his chest was sandwiched between the wooden boards. Then I wound the rope around his feet and legs over and over again. When he reached back to try to pull himself forward, I lassoed both his hands with the rope and tied them back to his ankles. Then I pushed a few loops of rope to the front, came out from behind the stairwell, and coiled the rope around his head and open mouth to stifle his screams. I knotted it tight behind his skull.

Just as I thought, the dude had a tattoo of a spider web that started at his left temple and filled down his neck and over his shoulder. It was impressive, as were the numerous tattoos all over his bare chest, legs, and arms. I grabbed the metal chair from under the stairwell, placed it at the foot of the steps just feet away from his head, and sat down.

"Look at you, Mr. Spider. Looks like I got you coiled from head to toe in my own web. How are you going to get out of this one?

He bent his head up slightly, which tightened the rope across the corners of his mouth. His eyes and forehead reacted to the pain as he let out a hard grunt.

"What's that? You want it tighter?"

He grunted again, rebellious pleading.

"I say I sit here for a few moments and observe my great handiwork."

For close to ten minutes I watched him struggle to break free. His feet and legs were so tightly bound by the rope behind the stairwell that he could only motion an inch or two to the left and right. I was merciless with the rope, not only coiling it tight around his ankles and feet, but weaving it in and around each toe. Then I looped it around a hook in the rafter, and ensnared his wrists and arms. Moving his legs pulled his arms tighter behind his back. Such wonderful pain caused by his own attempts to escape. When he finally exhausted himself, I removed my shoes and exposed my bare feet.

"Now that I got you in my web, Mr. Spider, I need to take a bite out of your neck. Let me show you how it's done."

With my arms draped over the back of the metal chair, I crossed my legs and extended my ankles out and around his neck. The tops of my feet pressed hard into his carotids as I locked my toes behind his head. His face instantly turned beet red.

"I'm choking you with my feet, Mr. Spider, in case you're wondering. Don't they smell nice? I can feel your neck pulse throbbing against my skin. It turns me on. Can you see what it's doing to me?"

I lifted his head up a bit with my legs so he could witness the bulge under my compression shorts. I reached under and stroked my cock a few times.

"That's right. This is what killing bad men with my legs does to me. And from the looks of what you got going on in this basement, and what I know about your housemate, you seem like another *very* bad man."

I tightened my ankles more, rubbed my bulge hard, and let out a satisfying moan while looking toward the ceiling. Sweat poured over his forehead, reflecting the light from the one dim bulb. Red dots exploded on his face as small capillaries burst. His eyes became narrow slits.

"Oh, your friend? I cracked his ribs tonight, collapsed his chest with these big hams of mine. I think he liked it." I rubbed my hands over my thighs and tightened my ankles again. "Too bad he could-n't be here to see what I'm doing to you now. I bet he'd get off to it too."

Mr. Spider let out muffled moans as the blood remained trapped within his head and was unable to circulate new oxygen into his brain. I held tight with the ankle scissor minutes after he passed out to make sure his kill was final.

A dead body makes a great practice dummy. I unencased Mr. Spider from his death cocoon and laid him out on the basement floor. Then I nestled down next to him, thinking of different ways I could take my next prey.

First, I slithered behind him, lifted up his torso, then crisscrossed my legs around his abs. His head swung onto my shoulder as I tightened my legs hard. His relaxed, gaping mouth echoed as the remaining air escaped. Then I raised my legs up to his chest and tightened my hamstrings around his ribcage like a thick piece of boat rope. As with his cohort, each of his ribs cracked one after the other. It aroused me to feel my thighs move closer together as his chest crumbled under the pressure. A little bit of blood escaped from his mouth.

It's either one of two ways I like to attack: the neck or the chest. I prefer the neck because I enjoy seeing a dude's face trapped so close to my cock. And I can feel the arteries in his neck pulsate against my hamstrings. It's intense to know I can maneuver all my leg muscles to control his blood flow at will. And his air intake. My thighs, my skin, my muscle fibers are like intricate sensors working together to provide the greatest death sensation.

What does it feel like for them? Dying by me. Like this guy tonight. I bet he didn't wake up this morning thinking he was going to be roped up and feet strangled. Somehow, I think he wanted it to end for him this way. Doesn't every guy?

I moved to the opposite end and sat between his legs. Then I grabbed his arms and pulled him back up so I could fit my ankles around his neck again. I outstretched my legs to see how tight I could get my feet. Not only did it feel nice, but it looked beautiful. If a living victim tried to break free, I'd just pull his arms back more and extend my legs. His own struggles would create a nice feet noose.

It's not gross or anything for me to test things out with a corpse. Not like I'm gonna have sex with it or anything. I just want to make sure the next guy can't escape whatever I may try. In a way, this one dude is providing a valuable service. I mean, I wanna cum right now. Always do after a kill. But then they'll track me down too soon. DNA and all.

It was close to 4 a.m., and I needed to move out before sunrise. I slipped out the basement window and maneuvered myself back to the van through bushes and small backyards. Once in my van, I stripped off my compression shorts and rested on the hard mattress. I had slipped in a DVD of a National Geographic special called *The Big Squeeze*.

For a full hour the film documented the life of a giant green anaconda. But there was one section that I liked the most: the part where the narrator says, "They crush their bones and suffocate them to death." This is the part that I looped. In it, a large anaconda encoils a deer or large mammal on the water's edge. Eerie but erotic music plays as they cut between a full shot of four large coils tightening around the prey's midsection, turning it in the process, and then a close-up of the coils around its hooves.

I sat there and drank a full bottle of wine, letting those words infiltrate my head as if I were succumbing to a cult-like trance. I wanted them to undulate in and out of every brain cell like the snake itself. "They crush their bones and suffocate them to death." I wanted to be fucked by those words. And with enough repetition, I would be.

An hour later I shot one the largest loads I can remember. It spewed out of me over and over again like a mechanical pump. I could almost hear it release. I didn't even care where it went. It would be dry by morning, and then I could plan my next kill.

Chapter 4

Woke up at 10 a.m. and the cops were already across the street investigating my first victim. Heard one say it was probably some gang-related shit. It's easy removing filth from the streets. They always thing it's other bad dudes that did it. Like some drug deal gone bad. Or just hangin' out with the wrong kind of people. This guy hung, all right, dangling between my killer thighs from a metal stair escape. I got a boner rethinking how I took him out hours ago.

Watching that video the night before of the large anaconda constricting its prey had me craving more. I couldn't get it out of my head. I slipped into a diner for a late breakfast to replenish my muscles— my legs muscles, to be exact. I wanted to focus on my next target, my next kill. How long would it take? Where would it be? I needed it so bad.

Drove back to Detroit the next day and hung out with some of my buddies from the dojo. We played around, of course. Helped keep my legs in good shape. Two weeks in I'm walking back from the gym and a large black Mercedes pulls up next to me. Guy rolls down his window. Asks me if I give private lessons. Thinks I'm some gigolo or something. He's wearing a suit. Forty-something, jet-black hair. White man, with a business arrogance about him. He cuts deals. Messes with people's money. Takes advantage of situations, then screws them over. One of those types. Prime food for a scissor killer, like me. So I say yes.

He took me up to his private suite. His name is Tom. At least that's what he says. Tells me to get comfortable on the sofa by the window. We're in the Renaissance Hotel, 33rd floor. The city lights reflect off the Detroit River. Sky is dark now, and you can see a storm rolling in. I lean back, prop my legs up, and listen as he works the phone.

He's talking lawsuits with a colleague. Forcing families to move out of their houses so a proposed development can go through. It's all in a day's work for him. Money-hungry man. Big dreams attained by big lies. That alone gave him part of what he wanted from me. My cock engorged at the thought of how I would take him, and before long his mouth was all over it.

He offered me a drink after ten minutes of sucking, and I asked for a shot of whiskey. There was a lot of booze on the glass and metal cart. I could tell he was a drinker. Maybe that's what it took to screw over others. A little bit of guilt relief? Or was it in celebration of another great deal? Either way, the effect on him made him more compliant to me, and he soon asked me to trap him between my legs.

It was midnight, and large drops of rain smacked against the window as the skies opened up. We were both naked by then. I had maneuvered him into a sitting reverse figure-four scissor. While he rested on his back, I wrapped my legs around his neck and sat up with my ass close to his face. He liked that position, evidenced by the twitching of his mediocre cock. I brought my thighs closer together and flexed my calves to make the hold tighter around his neck. His cock responded quickly.

In his inebriated state, he mumbled words that sounded like he wanted me to suck him off. That wasn't going to happen. I've always been the dominant alpha man, and nothing was going to change that now. Not even the $500 he offered for this night, which he laid out on the table in fifties like he was trying to impress me. Fucking corporate slug.

I like to play with my victims. Taunt them. In this case, I rocked my body back and forth, causing his head to lift slightly from the floor. I grabbed his balls tight in my large hands. He moaned in agony. He placed his hands on my thighs to feel the muscles. I flexed them several times to give him a good show. Then I went in for the kill.

I sat back and covered his face with my ass. He let go of my thighs and tried to stroke himself off, but I quickly grabbed both his wrists and held his arms away from his body. Then I cinched in my legs and tightened my glute muscles over his mouth and nose. He began to suffocate and tried to break free. But the booze and my thick body were too much of a match for him.

Suffocation is a hot word. It's like suffering and masturbation together. Suffocate. Suffocate. Suffocate. As I took this prey tonight, the words from *The Big Squeeze* film looped in my head. My legs were the coils around this deer's neck. And my ass muscles literally sealed his doom. It was the perfect hold, one I had never tried before. And he deserved it. He would no longer be making bad deals that ruined people's lives.

I pulled my hoodie over my head and exited the building a little after 2 a.m. My van was still in the gym lot a couple of miles away. Doug let me crash there between trips. He never knew just where I was going. He figured I traveled to check out other dojos and bring back new techniques. Bet he'd love the one I used on Mercedes boy, though we hadn't taken it that far before. I let him stroke himself in my triangle choke now and then, and he certainly enjoys watching my cock bulge against my face under my trunks. Still, there was a code of respect. I respected his free parking, and he respected my Herculean thighs.

I looped *The Big Squeeze* video again, hoping it would somehow hypnotize me while I slept. Maybe it would reveal new techniques to me. Ones I hadn't thought of. Ones that would make my future prey suffer even more. Then an idea for my next trip came to me the following morning, as if I were being guided by some hidden force within the video music. I would visit a herpetologist that studies giant snakes, and learn from the real thing.

Chapter 5

It was seven hours on the road before I entered the small town of Ashwood, Pennsylvania. Reptile World sat hidden within the mountains along a two-lane rural road. Tall trees formed a canopy above several indoor and outdoor enclosures. Seeing the large hand-painted snake that outlined the wooden sign above the entrance stirred something deep inside of me. I parked my van in the small dirt-covered lot and grabbed my camera.

Slick Rodgers was the curator for the collection of reptiles in the jungle-like sanctuary building just past the gift shop. Behind several acrylic housings were life-like replicas of tropical scenes. In them were native species: toads, lizards, turtles, and of course, snakes. Most of the snakes were small, venomous, no more than two to three feet long. They hid well among the various plant vines and natural settings.

I asked Slick if he had any large constrictor snakes. Told him I was from Michigan and researching mechanical ways of duplicating the pressure exerted by these enormous, sinewy creatures. Told him I had a friend who owned a few boas, but nothing more than six feet. He smiled and took me out back.

First we passed by several man-made "swamp" displays where a few alligators slept with their heads just above the water. Plaques along the sides detailed the various attributes and lifespans of these reptiles. The staff let them stay outside in the warmer months. One looked at me and turned its head slightly as I walked by. I knew what it was like to be a predator waiting for prey. I sensed it was hoping for another meal, as was I.

Slick took me to a far room where a large enclo-sure about 20 feet long and 10 feet wide housed this amazing specimen. "This is our largest constrictor. We call her Baby. She's a 26-foot green anaconda. Been with us for ten years now. Jim fed her a large pig last week that he purchased up the street from a farmer. You can see the bulge in her belly about halfway through." I took it that Jim was the snake's handler.

"We are thinking of simulating the pressure us-ing rubber tractor tire tubes filled with various sub-stances….air…water," I told him. It was all a big lie, as if I were an engineer or something. "What kind of pressure does a snake like that exert?"

"Full-on force was recorded with a gauge on a TV special I saw," he said. "They say the pressure is about equal to a bus sitting on your chest. People think they suffocate their prey, and that they do, but the pressure is so strong that it actually stops the prey's heartbeat. Stops the blood flow. Only takes a minute or two."

"So they are pretty efficient killers, yes?"

"I'll say, and they eat their prey whole, bones and all. Here, Jim will tell you more about them. I need to get back up to the front to greet more guests. We are a small attraction here in Pennsylvania, and visitors are our lifeline. Enjoy your time here."

Slick left and Jim came over to my side and shook my hand. We watched as Baby slowly slithered to a dark corner and curled in place.

"Big snake. Must be hard to handle," I said.

"She's actually pretty calm after she eats. I could go in there now and she will just shy away," Jim said.

"It must be pretty intense feeding the snake a whole live pig."

"This is nothing, man. I have a Burmese python at my place that's almost as long and eats twice as often. She's 24 feet now. Had her for nine years. Feed her every ten days. She's overdue for another feeding."

"So you have snakes at your house?" I asked.

"Yeah. I got a few boas too. Would you like to see them? I live about five miles away. I get off of work soon and thinking about having a beer and relaxing. I'll feed Diablo and you can watch. Diablo is the Burmese."

"Sure," I said. Jim was a small guy, about 5'5" and 140 pounds. Reminded me of the small dudes in the gym that I'd trap between my legs and lift up. Even looked a bit like one of them. "Let me follow you with my van."

Jim finished his daily chores and we left about twenty minutes later. While I waited, I flipped through some books in the gift shop—one titled *Tales of Giant Snakes*. I purchased it and followed Jim's lead when we exited the herpetarium. Slick had disappeared, so I wasn't able to thank him for his inspirational tour. If only he knew what was on my mind now, he might have thought twice about letting me in.

A bumpy dirt and gravel driveway surrounded by pine trees led me up to Jim's small cabin-style house set back from the road. He parked off to the side by an external building. I pulled my van up next to him and spoke out of the window.

"So, is this where you keep the monster snake?"

Jim laughed and nodded. "Yep, this is where she is."

"Good. I can't wait to see her."

I liked that this dude's place was hidden from sight. You could tell he was a snake enthusiast by his T-shirt: a large python coiled under the text,

"My Pet Can Eat Your Pet." And a sign above the entrance to the outer building read, "Beware of Snake."

Entering the snake enclosure was like walking into another environment. Higher temps and humidity immediately hit me. Like being in a jungle. It wasn't that big of a building, maybe 20 foot by 15 foot. There were three cage enclosures.

"This is my albino boa. He's eight feet long." Jim asked if I wanted to hold the snake. I let him drape it over my shoulder. Was nice feeling the smooth, rubbery coils of a constrictor against my body again. I liked how its tail coiled around my left bicep. The power in just one coil seemed impossible. It was all muscle: intricate body segments working simultaneously to provide maximum squeezing pressure. The perfect killing machine.

"You're a small guy, man. How can you even handle these snakes? Aren't you afraid of getting crushed yourself?" I asked.

"I've raised these ones since they fit in the palm of my hand. Never had any problems. Keep them fed and they leave you alone," he replied.

"Show me Diablo. I wanna see this big one."

Jim led me to the end of the building where Diablo lay along the back edge of the enclosure. It was a massive snake. The brown and black pattern of its shiny skin was mesmerizing. I wondered why it had that effect on me.

"Is this where you feed him too?" I asked.

"Oh yes, he likes it in here. She, I should say. Diablo is a female. Females are the larger in these kinds of snakes. But I like to think of her as a guy, cuz I like the name Diablo. The Devil Snake."

Jim smiled. I smiled back.

"What do you usually feed her?"

"Pigs, mostly. Dead ones. Frozen and thawed. Let me get the one I pulled out a few days ago."

"Will she attack dead prey?"

"Yeah, they strike and coil still. But they like live prey mostly. It's hard to raise pigs and other animals just for feedin'. So I get these from the farm for like one hundred dollars a pop." Jim unwrapped a package about the size of a small to medium dog. Inside were the raw, pink remains of the animal. It seemed like a small meal for a snake this big.

"I've seen videos of these kinds of snakes taking down full deer. Too bad you couldn't lure one inside. That would be something to see."

"This will last her for about a week," Jim said. "A deer could feed her for at least a month. Sure would be a lot cheaper too." Jim moved closer to the enclosure door. It was a large acrylic enclosure, almost like a giant terrarium. Large branches hung up to the ceiling with thick gobs of Spanish moss dangling from them. In the far corner was a round pool full of water. "Damn, it's hot in here. Grab you a beer?" Jim set the pig carcass by the door.

"That would be great. Let me go grab my phone. I want to film this."

As I made my way to the truck, I thought about the wonderful spectacle I was about to witness. I couldn't wait to see that massive snake tighten its coils around the pig. I wanted live prey, but I'd take what I could right now. When I returned, Jim had removed his T-shirt.

"Take your shirt off. Relax. I got us some chairs. Here's your beer." Jim popped the top off and passed it over. My first thought was to get him drunk and wrap my legs around his small, defined torso. Make him feel my pythonic strength. I needed to take another victim soon. But I resisted.

"How long does it take before he latches on to that thing?"

"Once I toss it in, shouldn't be but a few minutes. Diablo's a hungry one." Jim took a long swig of his beer. "You ready?"

"Go for it." I removed my shirt, drank some beer as well, and readied my phone camera.

Jim unlatched the lock on the acrylic door and quickly threw the still pig into the center of the enclosure. It made a loud thump on the moss-covered floor. Diablo lifted its head a bit and looked toward me through the clear sidewall. Jim latched the door shut and sat back down next to me.

I pressed record on the camera and waited a few seconds. Diablo flickered his tongue out to taste the air, then rested his head back onto his large coiled body.

"What's happening?"

"I don't know. Maybe he doesn't smell it yet. Give it a few minutes. When you see him start to move, turn your camera on again."

The two of us drank more beer and waited for about five minutes. Sweat dripped down our chests, which were illuminated by the large heat lamps inside the enclosure. I was fixated on the snake's body, as if it were my own. How I wish I could be that snake right now, stalking its prey. I wanted action. My cock pumped with excitement each time the snake moved a little. But it wasn't heading toward the prey. It nestled up tighter in the corner."

"Is it sick or something?" I asked. "Why isn't he going for it?"

"No, he...she's fine. I'll have to pour some blood or something on it so she'll pick up its scent. Let me see what I have.

The more I watched the snake ignore the dead prey in its confinement, the more I realized this was not what I wanted. Dark thoughts raced through my mind. We had both downed a second beer by now while waiting, and I felt a craving like I had never known. *The Big Squeeze* video of the anaconda coiling around the deer looped in my head, and I repeated to myself the familiar phrase: "They crush their bones and suffocate them to death." I said it out loud once when Jim returned.

"Here. I got us another beer. This should do it. Got a mixture of leftover roast beef gravy from last night. Let me spill some onto the pig in a second. You good?"

Both of us were burning up at this point. I rubbed the cold beer bottle over my forehead. "Yes. I'm good." I set the beer down and watched as Jim unlatched the enclosure door and stepped inside for the first time. The pig was maybe ten feet from Diablo's head. Jim drizzled the warm gravy all over the carcass while keeping an eye on his snake, accidentally spilling some onto his shorts and shoes in the process. When he walked back to the entrance, I had already closed and locked the door.

"What the fuck man?!" he said from inside. "Open the door up, dude. Not funny."

"No," I said, with my face pressed up to the acrylic. "I came to see a live feeding, and I'm not leaving without one." I stepped back and turned on my camera.

Diablo instantly sensed the movement within his enclosure. His tongue flickered several times as his head rotated around. Jim moved back to the door and tried to pry the lock open from inside.

"No use, Jim. If a snake that large can't escape, then neither can you. Mind if I finish your beer?" I pulled the neck of the bottle up to my mouth and smiled at the scene I had created in front of me. Jim began to panic.

"Take your pants off, and maybe I'll open the door."

"You're crazy! Let me out of here."

"I want to see you naked. Then I might think of opening the door."

"No way, dude! Open this damn door." Jim slid and fell from the gravy he had spilled by the pig.

I moved to the door with my camera and looked into his eyes as his breath formed a haze on the acrylic. "You do what I say. It's over for you. Face it. You've always wanted to feel the crushing power of these large snakes. You work with them all day. You are obsessed with them, like I am. This is your chance to experience it fully." Jim looked back and said nothing. I continued with my eyes deeply fixated onto his as if I were the snake coming toward him.

"You're *going* to strip fully naked for me, because Diablo takes his prey raw. He doesn't need to swallow shorts or boots. Take it *all* off."

Jim removed his boots and sat motionless in the far corner. By now, Diablo was almost upon the pig carcass. It was amazing to see this large pile of coils undulate and stretch out in length along the enclosure floor. The snake crept slowly, flickering its tongue with each push forward. Jim removed the rest of his clothing.

"Now rub some of that gravy from your shorts and feet all over you. Roll around in the bit you spilled by the door." I moved back to the side to get the full view of what was unfolding. "Go ahead, rub a little on your cock too. Looks nice and big now. I knew this would turn you on."

Jim followed my orders while he watched Diablo curve away from the still pig.

"He's coming for you. Or is it a she? Does it really matter at this point? You're about to feel the intense squeezing power of a giant Burmese python around your naked body. And I get to film it to enjoy over and over and over again. Maybe I'll post it to the internet to get other guys like us off. That would be nice, right?"

Jim nodded hypnotically. Diablo moved away from the pig and was now feet away from his live prey. Jim began to stroke himself.

"That's right, Jim. That's what you need to do. Build it up, but hold off. Don't ejaculate yet. Wait till Diablo is around you."

I took great pleasure in watching this giant snake about to snatch a big meal, and the build inside of Jim with his cock now engorged with blood. The alcohol and my coaxing convinced him to experience this fully. I stepped closer to capture the strike on video.

Milliseconds later Diablo lunged forward with the first four feet of his body, biting down hard in the middle of Jim's free forearm. Then, one after another, the snake's massive coils moved around Jim's naked body. The first two quickly encircled his bare chest, pinning both arms against his torso. The next set of coils weaved in and around his thighs just below his balls and cock. Then the weight of the coils forced Jim to his side, and Diablo began to wind around the entire length of his body.

Jim soon disappeared into a sea of brown and black-patterned coils that undulated along his body, tightening in the process. Within a minute only Jim's head, feet, and cock were visible. His feet protruded from the coils like the hooves of the deer in *The Big Squeeze* video. When the snake rolled him over one last time, Jim's face appeared within the light of the heat lamps. I zoomed in closer. His eyes were glazed over, and familiar red dots began forming on his face. He gasped a few times, letting out precious air that he would never get back. Each time he exhaled, the coils tightened in more, and it made me bone. The rippling effect of the coils gripping closer was mesmerizing. Then a coil slid up and around his neck, and I knew it would soon be over.

His eyes became slits, and strands of drool escaped from his mouth. In his final act of death, large loads of cum spilled from his cock as the thick coils pressed tightly against his balls from both sides. I reached down and stroked myself off after watching this amazing kill. It was the greatest release I have ever felt.

Chapter 6

ASHWOOD MAN SWALLOWED BY GIANT
BURMESE PYTHON.

That was the headline in the local newspaper a
week later. I had left the following morning and
stayed at a nearby hotel to figure out my next move.
I replayed the video of Jim being crushed over and
over again, and the aftermath that followed.

By 2 a.m. Diablo had maneuvered his head
down to Jim's bare feet. I watched as the snake's
mouth slipped over his toes. In a slow gnawing motion, Diablo ingested Jim's feet, then his calves,
then his thighs. It was incredible to see the snake
unhinge its mouth to the point that it could slide
over something as wide as a man's body. The thick
coils around Jim's chest and neck held him firmly
as the snake slowly pushed him inside from the
other end. As Jim's body bulge moved deeper, the
hypnotic black and brown pattern of Diablo's thick
skin stretched and rippled as if the snake were a giant rubber death tube.

When the snake's mouth moved over Jim's
torso, and slowly up to his neck, I could see what
appeared to be a smile on Jim's face. Certainly he
was dead by then, the lower parts of his body al-

ready dissolving in the snake's digestive juices. I know I was smiling, and aroused like never before. I slowly sipped four more beers from Jim's kitchen while savoring every second of the swallow. And after Jim's smiling head disappeared into the beast's throat hours later, I made sure to wipe away any of my existence there that night.

Heading back to Detroit soon after, I stopped at a restaurant just outside Canton, Ohio. Found myself hungry as ever for more meat. In this case, a New York strip at a restaurant dive where you toss peanut shells to the floor while you wait. I had already cracked open a dozen and washed them down with a glass of wine when I noticed a couple arguing a few tables away. Not out loud, but I could tell he was saying things that made her uncomfortable. He'd lean deep across the table and she'd cower with her head down to her plate. Then he'd sit back with a smirk on his face while he watched the effect of his words. Spousal abuse, not doubt. And she probably felt trapped in this loveless relationship.

My steak arrived twenty minutes later, and I dug into it like I hadn't eaten in days. As I chewed each piece, my eyes would rise over to the couple again. He was one of those redneck types, but not a good-ole boy. More like a player and a user. Someone who gets off on making others feel pain after he sucks them in with a bit of charm. Someone who takes advantage of people with empathy and compassion. And then his victims feel trapped, both emotionally and financially. It's a sick game that I've seen time and again. At one point he got up to use the restroom, and it was my cue to reel in another prey. I followed close behind.

I stood three urinals over and could hear him mumble words to himself under the cover of a tattered John Deere hat. His face was round with a bit of stubble outside of his thick brown mustache. Medium build, maybe a bit heavy in the gut. Stout legs, but not as thick as mine. And certainly not as powerful. I met him at the door when he recognized my Michigan State Wrestling T-shirt.

"They had a good season last year," he said. "We'll see what they can do next year."

"Yes. We'll see," I replied. I knew when someone wanted to get to know me, so I played his game. I gave him a nod and a smile and I was back at my table finishing my steak.

He remained quiet for most of the night, only shooting a few verbal daggers over to his girl that made her recoil each time. I could see he was looking my way now and then. I flexed my arms as I forked the remaining pieces of meat into my mouth to give him a good show. Felt like he wanted a challenge or something. I was up for it.

About an hour later, his girlfriend, or wife, got up to use the restroom. She should have made a run for it. He came over and stopped by my table.

"You wrestle in school?" he asked.

"Yes, I did. You?"

"I did when I was in junior high. Pretty good, I'd say. Used to beat the hell out of some of those guys. Get them in holds and not release. Make them cry like little babies after practice. That was the end of my wrestling career. Coach kicked me off the team. He was a prick anyways."

"That's too bad. I still wrestle. Do some jujitsu up at a dojo in Detroit when I get a chance."

"Why don't you come over to my place. Show me what you got. See if I can beat you in front of my girl. You'd like that, Tammy, right?"

Tammy had returned from the ladies room and "Bob" pulled her in by her waist, almost violently. "Go get me the bill," he commanded.

As she walked away, he made a comment that she could lose a few pounds in the hips and thighs. "Woman eats like a cow sometimes. Feel like I could put her out in her own pasture."

It was no surprise that Bob the abuser and Tammy lived in a mobile trailer park just a few miles from the interstate. Their unit was set back from the others and partially concealed by a row of unkempt bushes in front. The entrance faced the woods, where a faded awning barely held up over a makeshift patio. Two lawn chairs with a small table in between rested by an unused fire ring full of beer cans and cigarette butts. Bob and I sat down while Tammy retrieved some beers.

I'll skip past the small talk that ensued. Bob became overly confident and cockier with each sip. He repeatedly glared at Tammy whenever she came outside to join in the conversation. At one point he grabbed and twisted her wrist when she reached for empty beer bottles. "Don't you touch a damn thing, woman," he said. "Now stay the fuck inside. This is men time."

Bob cocked his head from side to side and his forehead crinkled when he told me about his wrestling days, like he was state champ or something. I was just searching for an in to get this kill started. I fantasized for a moment about drenching him with gravy and feeding him to Diablo the giant snake. Then it began to rain.

As I got up to leave, Bob tackled me from behind and we both fell to the ground. I wasn't really planning on leaving, but I knew that turning my back on this overzealous fool would get him to make the first move. I played along with our man-to-man romp until I was able to guide our bodies into the woods and away from where we could be easily seen.

The skies opened up and the torrential rain broke over mounds of dirt, forming a thick ooze of mud that pooled into a dip in the terrain. Bob the women abuser now became Bob the beast as he stripped off his shirt to reveal his broad chest. Two tattooed bands of barbed wire encircled his right bicep. I removed my wrestling T-shirt, popped off my shoes, and stepped barefoot into the satisfying sludge.

Bob lunged forward and our upper bodies clasped like the classic wrestler pose. Then he broke free and swung his big arms around my chest and locked his hands behind my back. His bearhug was tight, impressive. I could smell the booze on his breath and feel his groin press into mine. It was nice, actually. Nothing wrong with letting my opponent get the upper hand before I get the upper leg, so to speak. He held fast for almost a minute until we both collapsed into the thickening mud slurry.

I told him to remove his shoes and socks, and he quickly obliged. When there is mud, you gotta get raw. Out in the woods. Skin to nature. Two men wrapped tightly around each other. Bob had longed for this since his younger wrestling days. But he did the mainstream thing: got a job, got married, then tried to figure out what he really wanted in life. Certainly wasn't women, because he doesn't know how to treat them right. I don't feel sorry for him, though. Because he will never change. He's locked in his ways.

Bob heaved and gasped for air not more than three minutes into our rumble. No doubt due to heavy smoking. I rolled him around in a sleeper choke to exhaust him even more. Then I wrapped my thighs around his upper chest and locked my soiled feet together. It felt like bringing down a bull for the first minute, but I quickly wore him out.

I placed my muddy hand over his mouth and nose, and he began to shake with seizure-like movements. Then I released my legs from around his chest and moved them up to his neck. He bucked a few times like Jim's body did when Diablo was coiled around him. But that only lasts so long. My hamstrings cut into his carotids, and he soon became still. The moonlight reflected off my wet thighs and his contorted face. A few minutes later, he was dead.

As the rain subsided, I still held him tight. I didn't release my legs until an hour later. I liked how it looked, and how it felt. I could have slept there all night, in the mud. I felt like an animal. It was so primal. But I knew I needed to disappear.

At 5 a.m., just before daylight, I walked up to the mobile home and met Tammy, who had proba-bly watched the whole thing unfold. I told her she was free. She provided me with a shovel, and we both buried Bob the abuser farther back in the woods. Then she thanked me. I knew she wouldn't tell.

Chapter 7

The following day I was back in Detroit and at the dojo. The usual suspects were around, including Doug, who hit me up after class for some armless, face-to-crotch triangles. He asked me about the scratches on my thighs. I told him I had a rough outdoor brawl with a buddy. Then he sank his head back between my killer hams till I knocked him out a few times.

The TV in his office was on while we sat down for some food he had ordered from Berilli's Pizza down the street. News reporters talked about people on edge in the community with fires breaking out across town. Random homes and one business burned to the ground over the previous two weeks. Two people died in their sleep: a single mother and her daughter. Faulty wiring and a gas stove were to blame in two of the cases. But I had my suspicions.

"Horrible," Doug said. "I hope they find those fuckers doing this. I think it's arson."

The crimes didn't fit any pattern that I could see. May be drug related. Most things are these days. I needed to get my boys on lookout to help me catch this shithead or shitheads and introduce them to the heat of my thighs.

I sneaked in a short workout on the leg machines at the nearby gym before calling it a night.

Two days later I got word that one man was seen leaving the latest building fire on Woolworth Avenue. My street boys are always aware of their surroundings, and they feed me tips. They said it was a young man in his twenties, curly hair under his black hoodie, short, about 5'7". Said he was running down an alleyway about a block away. Disappeared into the darkness.

My dilemma: how do you catch an arsonist? How do I bait him? And how do I get to him before the cops do so I can work my mangle magic?

I parked my van within the vicinity of the latest incident and mapped out all four fires. The first was on 33rd and Washington Avenue. Second across town at 415 Mulberry Street. Third at 204 Westhausen. And fourth on Woolworth Avenue. Connecting the dots from first to last formed three legs of a star. My guess is his next strike will be somewhere near the corner of Haywood and Elmhurst Streets. And based on the time between the other fires, it would happen in two days. I had to set a trap, and quick.

On that evening I scoped out the area. Most of the houses along Elmhurst were vacant. The exact pinpoint on my map was a two-story derelict house with faded red paint on the wood siding. The screen in the front door was torn down halfway. A few old tires with grass growing up through them lay in the side yard. I grabbed them and took them inside. Only thing in the front room was a worn mattress on the floor and a few beer bottles. Looks like squatters moved on. Didn't appear to be anyone living there now.

The best access to the house without getting caught was along the back alley. I positioned my van a few houses down so I could see both ways through the tinted side windows. If he showed up at another house, I could quickly adjust my plan. But that was not the case.

Like clockwork, the dude showed up around 10:40 p.m. And just as I thought, he slipped inside using the unlocked back door. Before he entered, I saw a flash from a small can of some sort in his hand. Could be holding gasoline or another flammable substance. I had to move quickly.

When I heard a loud thump as I approached, I knew my trap had worked.

Inside, dude was lying on the floor. I had placed the large tires just above the second inside door and they came crashing down onto his head when he opened it. Metal rim must have hit him just right as he appeared to be knocked out. I pulled some rope out of my pocket and bound his arms behind his back. Then I grabbed his feet and slid him through the kitchen and onto the waiting mattress. I removed his shoes and tied his ankles together nice and tight. Finally, I applied duct tape around his head a few times to cover his mouth shut.

My cock was pulsing hard as it engorged with blood. A smile grew over my face like Kaa the giant python in *The Jungle Book*. I couldn't wait to squeeze this victim good and hard. He was such an easy catch. And now my legs would feast again. But first, I needed to figure out dude's motive for starting fires.

The flashing can was just as I thought: a bit of gasoline poured into a flask. Just enough to start a good fire with no evidence of a large can, which would have been noticeable from outside. A flask the police would assume was some remnant of a drunken person who crashed there.

I removed the dude's socks to reveal his bare feet. If he tried to make a run for it, the rusty nails and glass on the floor would slow him down. The mattress was the safe area. As he started to come to, I positioned my legs around his waist from behind and wrapped my arms around his neck nice and snug.

"Not so soon, boy," I said, as he awoke to his predicament and started to panic. I tightened my legs and pressed my bulge into his back. The air pushed out of him and silenced his attempts to make any noise.

"You listen to me," I continued. "You're not going anywhere tonight. You're going to stay right here with me as I work your body with my massive legs. Bones will break, ribs will pop, and your insides will collapse. And bloodbursts will form on your face when I tighten my thighs around your neck. I will cut off all air and blood flow, and you will die in my pythonic embrace. But *first*, you will tell me why you are setting these fires."

I placed my mouth close to his ear and whispered. "There is no escaping me." I removed the tape from around his head, and he let out a gasp. I loosened my constricting legs a bit so he could take in just enough oxygen to speak a few words at a time.

"Man, I can't man," he grunted. "They'll kill me."

"Who will kill you?" I said, while snapping my thighs together again.

"A cop. He is paying me. I need the money bad."

"What do you mean a cop?" I tightened my legs even more. "Tell me *everything*."

"They, they want these houses gone."

"Who wants the houses gone? The police?"

"No, the cop, he's helping some guy. Some guy with a lot of money. I don't know more than that."

"Who's the cop? Tell me!" I crushed again, and one of his ribs started to creak.

"I don't know his name. He's white. Heavy. He told me if I don't help him he'll put my in jail for robbing a store. They have video of me."

"And what happens if you don't burn down this house tonight?"

"They will find me. They will send me to jail, or even worse, kill me!"

At this point I wanted to completely crush the fuck out of this dude, but something told me I could use him to get even more kills. I needed to expose this cop he was talking about, and get to the bottom of this all.

"You killed a woman and her daughter! Did you know that?"

"No, no, I didn't mean to! The fire I started next door traveled to their place before the firefighters could get there. They told me nobody would get hurt."

"Who told you?"

"The cop."

"Are any firemen in on this?"

"I don't know. I don't know!"

I cinched my arms tight around the dude's neck and flexed my biceps into his carotids. Within seconds he was out cold again. I had to give myself time to think. Time to figure this one out.

As the night lingered into the early morning hours, I held tight to my victim. When he came to, I told him *exactly* how he was going to work for me. I told him that if he did not cooperate, me and my boys would track him down and far worse things would happen to him. I reminded him over and over again of the power of my legs. At one point I held his neck deep within my hamstrings and made him pass out with his face against my bulge. The smell of my sweaty crotch would intoxicate him, seduce him, hypnotize him, and make him comply with my commands. I repeated this over and over again, making him pass out and come to nearly five times. I felt like Kaa seducing Mowgli, the jungle boy. I wore him down nicely.

By 4 a.m. I led the kid to my van after unbinding his feet. Then I fed him some food and we talked about how he would tell his "boss" the next day that the fire didn't take this time. That he would try again the following night. And that before he set another fire, he wanted to meet with the cop to collect his pay.

I would watch and film from my van. I would witness the pay deal go down. And I would have something on the cop. Something he wouldn't want anyone else to know. And he would be my next victim.

Chapter 8

At exactly 10:45 a.m. the next day, I had the dude, who went by Franco, call the cop. I recorded it all. He told him that the house did not catch and to meet him at another location to pay him for more fires. It was a long shot. I figured the cop would want to keep it all clean and all, and make as little contact as possible. But this one was stupid.

I picked out a small warehouse about three blocks away from the recent target. Two stories, brick, dingy outside, some broken glass. An old building. Probably built in the 1950s. Inside there were old packaging machines probably unused for decades. And in the back, a room with wall-to-wall cement and a deadbolt lock from the outside. It would be the perfect place to hold this man hostage and *squeeeze* out the information I needed to track down his principal contacts.

We dragged the mattress from the abandoned house into the "cell" room in the warehouse. With so many vacant houses in that area, there was no one around to witness our actions.

At 12:15 p.m., this cop showed up in a sporty new Acura LX with gold tire rims. The car stood out from the backdrop of dilapidated buildings and cracked asphalt. He was in plain clothes, a wise choice for an otherwise stupid action. I remember the guy as soon as he stepped out of the door and ground his cigarette into the pavement. Some cop that came on the force before I left. Randy was his name. He seemed kind of cocky, rogue. Belly on him. Out of shape. I figured he wouldn't last long. And if I have anything to do with it, he won't be going home any time soon.

I slipped on my black luchador mask an opponent at the dojo turned over to me when he lost a bet to take me down. Guy couldn't stand a chance with my meaty thighs wrapped around his torso while in my guard. Every time I slip on that mask—and peer through the gold-lined eye holes—I think about how much it aroused me to watch his chest compress under the pressure, and to hear him beg for mercy while wheezing for air.

But this time I wore it to hide my identity. I couldn't risk having the cop flee and tell everyone who I am. Up to this point I've escaped any kind of national notoriety for my suffocatingly savage scissor spree. All my other victims were mostly deadbeats anyways—criminals, low-lifes. Except for the guy I fed to his python. I wonder if Diablo has shit him out yet.

From one of the warehouse windows, I filmed Franco meeting the cop near the front of the building, and exchanging payment. I told Franco to keep his phone in his pocket to record the audio. A money shot alone wouldn't be incriminating enough. I needed something to hold against him. To remind him that we had him trapped.

Franco's next move was to get the cop into the warehouse entrance, just inside enough for me to nab him. But it seemed to be taking longer than I thought. For a moment the two appeared to be walking over to the house from last night. I was afraid Franco was going to bail on me and reveal my plan. But he stopped the cop midway and said something to make him turn around. Then they were headed back to the warehouse, so I had to get into place quickly.

Now they were close enough for me to hear their conversation. They stopped by the door entrance. Franco was telling the cop that he thought he saw someone go into the house before the cop arrived. And that it would be safer to talk inside the building. And to tell him what happened the night before. And "maybe the warehouse would be a good location for me to hide out between fires." The sucker took the bait.

Franco pushed open the heavy metal door and a shaft of bright light momentarily surged across the dirty cement floor. When the door closed, I lowered myself from a rope like Spiderman and instantly ensnared the cop's head into a figure-four scissor. As he grabbed for my legs and struggled, I held tight onto the taut rope, which connected to a pulley above. Franco flipped a switch and the rope began to raise a few feet, just enough to keep the cop on his tiptoes and for me to cinch my calves and thighs tighter. It was a beautiful leg noose. As the cop began to lose consciousness, he swayed back and forth like a pendulum, his shoes dragging over the floor and etching out a circular pattern within the debris. It took all but thirty seconds to knock him out.

I unleashed my legs and wound a spool of rope around the cop's arms and chest as tight as I could. Franco removed the gun from the man's waistband and held it on him.

"He's out cold now," I said. "Help me get him into the room before he comes to."

Once the rope was knotted, I pulled my latest catch across the warehouse while Franco lifted his feet. He was a heavy man, probably around 250 pounds. It was a large haul, for sure.

I laughed. "We should tie his wrists and ankles around a thick stick and carry him like they do in the jungle movies. That would be a sight. You like jungle movies, Franco? Tarzan?"

Franco seemed a little nervous about the whole situation. "Man, this is crazy. The other cops are going to come looking for him. And then we're dead!"

"Relax, kid. I got his phone. And give me your phone with the recordings."

After setting the cop down on the mattress, I had Franco duct tape his mouth. Then we shut and locked the door.

"Okay, next we have to bring his car inside from the back. You do it, Franco. And if you try making a run for it, think twice. I have video of you now accepting money for your crimes, and it probably wouldn't look too good getting caught on the streets in a cop's car."

Franco complied, as I knew he would. He pulled the car through the back loading dock and we locked all the doors. Mission accomplished.

Soon after, I removed my mask and sat in a chair directly in front of Franco, who was leaning against a shrink-wrapping machine.

"Randy. His name is Randy Sawyer. That's right." I scrolled through the cop's phone, which I had unlocked using the man's fingerprint. I disabled the security and location settings. "There, now we wait and see who contacts him. His schedule says he's off duty till Monday. Are you hungry?"

"Yes, I'm starving."

"Good. Let's go get some grub and bring it back here. It's gonna be a long few days."

We returned with a couple of subs from Gerino's, a small sandwich joint two miles away. I heard the cop's phone ping a few times on the ride back. Once I had my van concealed within the warehouse, I got out and checked it.

One text was an appointment from a dentist. Another from a car repair shop. I scrolled through and read a few others, going back a few weeks. Nothing seemed suspicious, although there was one cryptic message from a guy named Wade. It read, *"We're still on schedule to approach the City Council. We're counting on you to make this happen."*

Why would they want to approach City Council? Could it be something pertaining to the police force? Like a pay raise or headquarters relocation? I checked the number. It belonged to a developer named Wade Provenzano.

I sat down and took a large bite out of the Italian sub I ordered. Franco seemed a bit more relaxed after eating his.

"Who are you, anyways?" he asked.

"I'm the guy that's going to get you out of this mess. Come over here."

Franco pulled his chair next to mine and sat down.

"Now feel the muscles in my legs."

He reached over and slightly grazed his hand over them.

"No, I mean *grab* them and *feel* them." Franco gave my right thigh a good squeeze.

"I saw how you knocked that guy out. It was like watching a superhero movie. They're incredible."

"That's right they are. You know what comes with these thick thighs and bulging calves?"

"No, what?"

"Justice. Justice is *served* in the *curves* of my legs." I laughed.

"I thought you were going to crack my ribs last night. I've never felt so much pressure..."

"I *will* crack your ribs, and knock you out again. It's just something you're going to have to get used to while you work with me. I need to keep them in good shape. So from now on, you're my practice dummy. I few broken ribs is a lot less painful than twenty years in the penitentiary."

Just then the cop's phone pinged again. And up popped a text from the Wade number.

"Randy, we need them cleared faster. We may lose our investors, and then this whole thing could come crashing down on us. I'll be watching the news."

Bingo.

Chapter 9

It was 8 p.m. when I slipped on my luchador mask again and opened the metal door to the room where our cop lay on his side on the mattress. His breathing was shallow, no doubt from struggling to break free from the many winds of rope around him. I walked over and squatted down in front of his face so he could see my legs.

"Just checking in on ya, buddy. Name is Randy, I see. You hungry?"

Randy nodded quickly several times. Then he took a deep breath through his nose and murmured something unintelligible through the duct tape still over his mouth.

"Now then. We are going to have to make a deal here. If I remove that tape, you are to remain quiet. No outbursts. No yelling." I cupped his chin and pulled his face toward my knees. "Understand me?"

Randy nodded quickly again.

"Good. We're gonna have a nice long talk." I braced the side of his face against my calf muscle and unwound the duct tape. Pieces of his hair stuck to the underside as I pulled off the final length. Randy gasped a quart of air and rolled onto his back.

"That's right. Catch your breath. Feels nice to get a little more air in those lungs, yes?" I stood up and circled the mattress. "Take it all in while you can."

I called Franco over when I reached the open door.

"Franco, bring those two folding chairs in here."

Franco immediately rounded the corner, but hesitated for a moment when he made eye contact with the cop. We positioned the chairs in the near two corners of the room entrance and sat down.

"Franco has been telling me a lot about you, Randy."

Randy's eyes shifted to Franco.

"He's *my* boy, now," I continued. "He works for *me*. That right, Franco?" I shot a controlling glance at Franco, who nodded obediently.

"Yes, sir."

"And he's been telling me that you've been paying him to torch down these abandoned houses." I stood up and maneuvered my chair closer to the mattress for an interrogation of sorts. "What I want to know is, why is a cop paying him to do so?"

Randy caught his breath, then looked defiantly back at me. "I don't know what he's been telling you, but I haven't told him to do anything."

"Oh, is that so?" I looked over at Franco, who wanted to speak until I waved him off. "I think you're not telling me the truth, Randy. I think you are involved in some sort of business deal." I pulled out his phone from my pocket. "While you were knocked out, I used your finger to unlock it for me."

"Remove this rope from around my chest!" Randy struggled to break free for a few seconds. "I'll have you both arrested!"

"Struggle all you want. You're not getting free from here. Are you going to tell me who Wade is?"

"I don't know what you're talking about! Who are you, anyway? You're in some serious trouble for kidnapping me."

"By the looks of it, I'd say you're the one in trouble. No one expects you back on the force for a few days, your car is locked inside this abandoned warehouse, and you're tied up tight in a soundproof room. Franco, go grab that bottle of whiskey I bought out of the van."

I kneeled on the mattress behind Randy and wrapped my left arm tightly around his forehead. Franco returned with the bottle. "Here, while I pull back his head, you put the bottle in his mouth and tilt up." Randy tried to shake my arm free, which only made me cinch my thick bicep tighter. "Open your mouth. You have no choice."

Franco dug the neck of the bottle inside the cop's lips and lifted the end. "Not too much," I said. "We don't want him choking on it. Randy, take it in. It will make you feel better."

Franco did as I said, then removed the tip of the bottle as I pushed Randy's head forward. Randy coughed a few seconds, then breathed slowly.

"There you go. Franco, do it again." I pulled Randy's head back one more time and he downed another gulp. "We got a lot left in this bottle, and a long night ahead of us."

By 10 p.m. Randy's eyes were glazed over. He could barely hold his head up. We fed him some of the leftover sub before he passed out onto the mattress. This guy was going to be hard to crack.

As midnight approached, both Franco and I had drank nearly half the bottle of whiskey. My thighs were raring to feed, and my eyes began examining his short, slender body. As we spoke, I found myself rubbing my hands over the sides of my quadriceps. I could feel my hamstrings, which were as taut as steel cables. I could easily take this boy out, but I needed him to solve this case.

"Hey Franco, come over here. Pull your chair close to mine. Feel this."

Franco slid closer, almost tipping his chair over in the process. He was clearly under the influence of the whiskey. Or maybe my legs. Or maybe both.

"Feel my adductors when I flex." Franco put his hand between my thighs. "Tight, right?"

Franco smiled a silly drunken smile. "Yes, you are very strong."

"How would you like to feel those around your neck right now?" I didn't give him a chance to respond.

"Here, sit down in front of my chair facing me." Franco took another swig from the bottle and plopped himself down. His head swung slowly from side to side before he looked up to the warehouse ceiling as if eyeing the heavens. Then he lowered his head back down to me.

"Man, I am wasted as fuck," he said.

"Good, that's the way I want you. I want you feeling good all the way through. I want your head buzzing." I propped both my calves against each side of his neck. "Move forward a bit."

Franco shuffled closer, just enough for me to lock my ankles together on the other side of his neck. I pushed my calf muscles into his carotids and flexed a few times. Franco's face turned red almost instantly.

"Now try to pry my legs free."

Franco reached around and grasped my shins. His efforts to move them apart were futile. They didn't budge an inch. In retaliation, I squeezed tighter and held it on him for twenty seconds.

"It's all about controlling your oxygen and blood flow. Control the head, control the body." I let loose for a second, then pumped my calf muscles deeper into his neck. He passed out momentarily, and his arms fell to the floor. I continued to hold his head up in my leg scaffolding until he came to.

"What…what. Damn. Did I go out?"

"Yes, you did. Feels nice, right?"

"My lips are numb. Haha."

"I want you addicted to that feeling. Have another shot of whiskey."

I released my legs from Franco's neck so he could reach over to the bottle on the warehouse floor.

"This shit is good." Franco took a long swig.

"That's right. Get the head buzz going. Not too much. Let me work that into you. Move closer to my chair."

This time I locked Franco's head between my lower thighs. I rubbed my hand through his curly hair before I squeezed my quads together. Franco's head rose up when my thigh muscles sank under his chin.

"I won't hurt you. Just yet. You know I can. I just want you to feel the pleasure of it all."

"Do it. I want it." Franco smiled in his inebriated state. I flexed my thighs nice and slow until I could feel his neck vein pulsating against my skin. Then I held him there. Soon his eyes became slits, looking back at me in the euphoria of asphyxiation I've seen on other men so many times. Like Doug from the dojo, and all the men that I've killed so far. But Franco wouldn't die tonight. He was too valuable to me now. And I enjoyed having him completely under my spell.

I carried Franco's limp body to my van and laid him along my narrow mattress. He was out cold. I took his shirt and shoes off, and stripped him to his boxers. After drinking another shot of whiskey out on the chair, I returned to the van and took off all my clothing. I slid behind Franco with my back against the van wall. My arms naturally encompassed his neck in a loose sleeper hold. And my legs circled around his waist with my ankles criss-crossing in front and pressing into his groin. I wouldn't be sleeping alone tonight.

At 3:00 a.m., Franco awoke for a bit. I could feel his limbs shuffling around. I immediately tightened my grip.

"Where am I?" he said.

"You're with me, sleeping in the van."

"Please don't kill me," he said in a shallow breath.

"I'm not killing you. I'm making you mine."

I flexed my biceps tight around Franco's neck until we both fell asleep again.

Chapter 10

Franco reminded me of this dude I wrestled in school. David was his name. Scrappy kid that liked to horse around with the other guys after practice. Always trying to get something going.

One Saturday night, after a meet, he stayed around in the locker room after all our teammates had left. It was a home match. I beat my guy in the first round. Pinned him with my legs weaved around his arms. That was the most you could use your legs in freestyle wrestling. Scissors were not allowed anymore. Anything that causes long-lasting pain. What a shame. That's why guys took to their spare time to try them on each other.

So Franco caught me coming out of the shower as I rounded the corner. He was goofing around with his gym bag while sitting on the bench. I hardly spoke to him much; I was more into scoping out dudes in my weight class. But there he was, all alone.

I knew. Of course, I knew. He had a thing for me. Who wouldn't? I was the star jock on my team. I always won my matches, and I oozed masculinity. Sometimes I'd grab my balls after a win, and coach always told me not to do that again. But I did. Every time. Until they got used to it. I think fans started looking forward to my signature move.

David wanted me. He was too shy to approach me around the other guys. But here he was on that day, growing some balls and finding a way. Just hanging around a little later than normal, like many guys with his desires did at schools all around the country. I commend him for that. Takes a lot of guts. So I couldn't let him down.

I toweled off slowly, and didn't make any attempt to hide my naked body as I slipped into my workout shorts. Then I tossed him one of those guy nods, and he said, "Great meet."

"Damn right it was," I replied.

"Coach asked me to lock up."

"Ah, so you're waiting for me to get my shit together and get out of here?" I said.

"No, no, take your time. I ain't goin' anywhere."

I rubbed my bare chest with the towel and threw it his way. It landed over his head. I laughed a bit, and so did he when he took it off.

I walked over and picked up the towel, then slowly wrapped it around David's neck. I pulled the ends tight while he gazed up at me.

"You wanna hit the mats with me, boy?" I said. "Just you and me, right now?"

And that's when I realized the power I had over other guys. David let me destroy him in ways he would never allow in a real match. I dished out scissor holds every chance I got. I scissored his arms behind his back and crisscrossed my ankles around his neck at the same time. I scissored his abs while locking him in a full nelson from behind. I reverse scissored his head and pulled my foot back till his face was buried in my ass. I think he enjoyed that one the most. Then I finished him off in a sleeper/scissor combo with my thighs tight around his chest.

"Having a hard time breathing there, David?" I sunk it in deeper till he passed out. By the time he woke up, I was already outside the door. I bet he thinks about that night a lot, even today.

Franco and I came to just a bit after 10 a.m. Both of us were a little drowsy from the night before. Whiskey can take a lot out of even the toughest men. We fed the cop a bottle of water before heading out for more carry-out subs. In the middle of eating mine, a text from Wade popped up on Randy's phone.

"I didn't see anything on the news today or last night. Get in touch with me ASAP."

I showed Franco. "Tell me more about what you know."

Franco swallowed a bite from his meatball sub, then wiped his mouth. "He told me to torch down a house a night. And to make it look like a star pattern. I heard him mention something about star entertainment or something."

"What does City Council have to do with all of this?"

"I don't know. Maybe text back like you're Randy. See how they respond."

"I say we make another attempt to *squeeeze* more information out of the cop first. Care to watch?"

"I'd love to. Put your thighs around his neck like you did me last night."

Back at the warehouse both Franco and I entered the secluded room after I put on my mask and stripped down to only my black compression shorts. Randy was snoring on his side until we propped up his body. The rope was still tight around his chest and arms, revealing indent marks on his skin from when he shifted around. I removed the tape from his mouth and placed my chair at the edge of the mattress. Franco kneeled behind him to keep him steady while I locked my legs around Randy's neck. This would be round two of my interrogation.

"You're looking a little groggy there, Randy? Last night's whiskey a little rough on the body?"

Randy looked at me in a semi-defiant manner...until I started to squeeze. Then his facial expression changed. I saw fear in his eyes.

"Now I, or rather you, got a text from Wade this morning. Tell me why he is having you burn down these houses." I applied more pressure.

"I, uh, don't know why."

"Liar!" I pumped my hamstrings into his carotids for a few seconds so he could see I wasn't joking. "No good cop would allow that."

Randy's fat face puckered up and turned two shades of red darker. My cock reacted on cue. Franco handed me Randy's phone.

"Let me turn on the camera app here and take a picture. What would the guys on the force think of your neck trapped between a man's legs in an uncompromising position?" I snapped a picture of Randy's face with my boner in the foreground. Then I showed it to him.

"See. You look good. Like you're enjoying it. You *are* enjoying it, right Randy?" I throttled my thigh muscles in and away from his neck.

"Stop! Please...stop."

"Are you ready to confess?"

"Yes, I'll tell you." Randy's eyes looked like they were about to roll back into his head.

"Let me get this on video. Now go. Tell me."

"Wade is a developer. One of his clients is Star Entertainment." Randy paused to catch his breath. "They want to build casinos in that area. But City Council won't rezone it. So he made a deal with me to scare them into reconsidering by burning down houses. Already some of the nearby tenants have moved out. There is a lot of money involved."

"And how much is he paying you?" I snapped my thighs back together around his neck and face.

"Two hundred fiffty thousand."

"Fifffty thousand? What's the matter, cat got your tongue? Hard to speak when your head is in a leg vise grip."

Franco reacted. "What? You only paid me $100 per house and you're getting a quarter of a million dollars!"

"That's a large sum of money, Randy. How much has Wade paid you so far?"

"He's given me $20,000. All we needed was three or four more houses, and then I'd get the rest. Star Entertainment would be able to convince the City that the casinos would be a better use of the land."

"By pushing people who can barely scrape by to live where? In the streets?"

Randy was silent for a moment. "I could split the money with you."

"Hell no! You're lucky I haven't killed you by now." I resumed my leg torture and Randy cried out in agony.

"I got all I need to know for now. Franco, give him some water and the rest of my sub." I released my legs from Randy's neck and exited the room. After Randy finished eating, Franco took him to the bathroom in the corner to take care of his business. Then he returned him to the mattress and locked the door.

I studied Randy's phone for the next few hours. I used Wade's full name to track down his whereabouts. Social media posts for his business revealed that he would be in Chicago Monday morning to unveil a new tech center.

"*Wade*," I typed on Randy's phone. "*Let's get together. I have some good news to share.*"

It wasn't long before Wade texted back. "*City Council cave? I'll be in Chicago next week. Meet me there. I'll be staying at the Marriott on 3rd and Grant. Room 322.*"

"*Okay, I will see you there.*"

Wade was about to get a good taste of the Scissor Killer.

Chapter 11

I made Franco stay with the cop while I was away. The boy was completely under my control now. I gave him some money to feed himself and to watch over the room. He knew when I got back there'd be much more of me in his life, legs and all. I was growing fond of this arsonist turned vigilante side-kick.

I packed the van with some *supplies* and drove out of the warehouse in the dark early hours of Monday morning. I'd be in Chicago before noon, and could scope out the hotel. I devised my plan as I drove along I-94 across Michigan.

This multi-tiered operation had many wrongdo-ers. You had Franco setting the fires. Then the cop profiting from it. And a developer trying to get his cut from an entertainment company. I'm pretty sure it stopped there. Wade would be the first to fall prey to my scissor justice.

It had been over two weeks since I had killed with my legs. Woman-abuser Bob was probably decomposing nicely in the woods behind that trailer park. Tammy probably had a new man by now. I felt good about what I did there.

Working the cop and Franco to the brink of death satisfied my cock, to some extent, but not my passion to take someone out whole. I needed that. Wade would be a few days off. I'd have to be careful with that one and keep myself incognito until the time was right.

At 4 a.m. I pulled over to a rest stop near Gary, Indiana. I needed to piss and grab some snacks. I hadn't had time to stock up my van fridge. Saw only one other car there, a beat-up green sedan. Rust bucket. Didn't see anyone around. Pissed my load in the urinal and exited to the vending machines. Only one dim bulb still working above, so I could barely make out the selections. Pushed the button for some cheese crackers, then felt the end of a gun pressed into my temple.

I couldn't wish for anything better.

My instincts and martial arts skills told me to move as quickly as possible to disarm an assailant. So I shot my arm around and knocked the gun free from his hand, then carried a punch to his face. He fell to the cement floor instantly.

Another thug, not too big of a guy. Down on his luck. Had to resort to mugging rest-stop people to carry on with his drug habit, or whatever. I didn't care. I didn't give a fuck. All I knew was that my crotch needed a good feeding, and his body would make the perfect meal.

So I grabbed him by his feet and dragged him to the back. He started to come to when my thighs were already snug around his waist, facing me. I wanted to see the look in his eyes as I snuffed him out.

The first pop sent a shockwave to my cock. One rib broken. The second made my head rush. Then I took out a third, and a forth. His ribcage was collapsing like dominos falling, one by one. He tried to scream, but my big hands tight around his neck prevented his vocal chords from making much more than a squeal sound. Then I figure-foured his waist with my legs. Total surround connection, like the coils of a large snake. I was now Diablo.

I held him tight. No releasing. I showed no mercy. He raised his torso up as if his soul was already leaving his body. The grimace on his face made me want to continue this torture forever. I squeezed tighter than I ever have. His eyes rolled back into his head minutes later. And not long after, he was dead. I shot a load inside my pants.

I dragged his body far back into the woods behind the rest stop. No one would ever check there. Found a soft spot and buried him a few feet underground with the shovel I had retrieved from my van. This is what happens to bad people—the ones that choose the wrong path. They are forlorn. Ghosts, essentially. Separate from society by their own dumb choices and misdoings. No one will care about this guy. He will soon be forgotten. But not by me. He will be another great kill that I loop in my head for years to come.

I took my time the rest of the way to Chicago. I figured I'd toy with Wade. Send him text messages from Randy's phone as I got nearby. Maybe make him go out of his way to see me.

This new tech center will probably be standard fare for him. Nothing spectacular. Just another four-story building lined with newly planted trees in mounds of mulch that look like mini volcanoes. You know the type. I despise those kinds of developments.

According to his social media posts, it was more of a groundbreaking ceremony. He'd attend, cut the ribbon with city representatives, then be on his way. The next day the heavy machinery would come in and lay the foundation. This gave me a sinister idea.

I arrived in Chicago just after noon and pulled out Randy's phone.

"Wade, I've just entered the city. But I want to avoid getting caught on hotel security cameras when we talk. Meet outside somewhere more secluded?"

It was almost an hour before Wade texted back.

"I'm attending a ribbon-cutting ceremony at a job site this afternoon. It's outside of the city about ten miles. Wooded area cleared for new develop-

ment. I'll text you when the ceremony is over and you can meet me there. I'll give you directions then."

I knew the address of the job site. It was clearly outlined on his social itinerary: *134 Westwood Avenue.* I'd make my way there after eating lunch. I was going to need the strength for what I had in store for him.

South Chicago, where I was currently sitting in my van at a convenience store, reminded me of the worst parts of Detroit. Driving up one of the residential streets I thought I saw kids playing around a dead dog. It certainly wasn't sleeping. There were rows after rows of turn-of-the-century brick houses that looked like something out of the apocalypse. Probably nicer back in the day, when times were a lot better for our country. More prosperity. Families happy to have their own homes. Now it's turned to shit.

I slipped into the store and picked up a few of those pre-made sandwiches with thinly cut deli meat and cheese that has no taste. And some bottles of sports drink and water. Hadn't eaten well since steak night at that Ohio restaurant where I met Bob the wrestler/abuser. Man, I have to admit. Killing him with my mud-caked legs in the pouring rain was a big turn-on. I thought about that as I scarfed the sandwiches and washed them down with Fierce

Blue Cherry Gatorade. It was like I was consuming his lifeless body. It made me hard.

Afterward, I drove closer and closer to the job site. My intention was to scope out the place from a distance and figure out how I wanted to take Wade down. From his pictures online, he would be an easy kill. Probably 5'9", 150 pounds. Older guy, like in his late fifties. Had that cocky look of prestige and money. Bet he doesn't live in a row house. No, probably one of those mansions in Gross Pointe. Funny, isn't it? How developers will overbuild in some areas, making it harder for the rest of us to get around. Then they'll live somewhere as far away from that as possible. Like in the country with their sprawling estates and open land. We get stuck with asphalt and small mulch trees. Greedy fucks.

I grew up in one of those bad areas in Detroit. You learn to be tough. You learn to not take shit from anyone. You become a badass to survive.

Wrestling was my outlet. And becoming state champ lifted me up. But I never forgot my roots. That's why I joined the local police force. But like this guy Randy that I currently have tied up in a Detroit warehouse, there were a lot of bad seeds in the department. I guess they felt it wasn't worth it after a while. Burnt out. Some even in the drug trade themselves. That's why I left. And that's why I'm taking the law into my own hands. Or in my case, my own *legs*.

I gave Franco a call with my phone to see how things were going back there.

"Hey man, I'm here in the city. How's our captive?"

"Hey! He's fine. I think he's still recovering from the whiskey a bit. Haha. I think I am too."

"Okay. Nobody's come around the place? No strangers?"

"Nope. I woke up to a siren going down the street, but that's about it."

"Dude, I almost got mugged at a rest stop. I took the guy to the back and snuffed him with my legs. Crushed his ribcage."

"Oh shit. That's awesome. I wish I could have seen it. I like watching you torture guys. Maybe you can teach me."

My first instinct was that Franco might make a run for it as soon as I left. But then I realized he had nowhere else to go. And holding him tight within my arms and legs at night gave him comfort.

"All right, boy. You stay off drinking until I get back later tomorrow. Grab some of those iron plates by the machines and do some lifting. I want you pumped up and ready to go. I have plans for you."

Chapter 12

It was 3 p.m. when the groundbreaking ceremony began. I parked my van across the street in a vacant lot that used to be an old gas station. As I peered through my side window with binoculars, a small crowd formed on the clay lot in front of me. About a dozen or so people arrived: men in dress pants and women in skirts. And a photographer guiding them where to stand. Plus some city representatives, I'm sure.

And then there were the shovels, seven neatly aligned in a row. One of them would be Wade's. Probably the one in the center. I would watch his movements carefully. I'd have to remember that I am Randy, coming to talk to him.

Wade showed up in jeans, the expensive kind. And a dress shirt. And a pair of expensive boots. Trying to look younger than he really is. Standing there all smug as the photographer took several pictures from different angles. All with a backdrop of pristine woods now with a big chunk removed.

Was I wrong to want to kill this man? No. His fate was decided when he chose to do what he did in Detroit. Have fires set to scare residents. Build at any cost. All for profit's sake. Like the guy in the business suite that I suffocated to death, people like this are just as guilty of crimes against humanity as rapists and murders. Their tactics alter lives forever.

Building a casino in my home area might bring in jobs, but it would also lead to gambling addictions, alcoholism, and despair. It would tear apart families, and destroy the fabric of the community, tattered as it is. Fix what we have, provide people with better jobs, and encourage small, locally owned businesses. Give people hope.

As the wave of ceremony goers parted and entered their cars, I watched Wade pace back and forth along the empty development. He was alone and looking at his phone. Within seconds a text popped up on Randy's phone.

"Where are you?"

I grabbed the phone and texted back.

"I'm in the white van across the street from you."

Wade looked up and then back down at his phone.

"Come meet me in the field here. Everyone is gone."

"I'd feel better if you came to me. I want to keep our meeting secret. It's very important."

Wade shook his head a few times before typing back.

"Okay. I'm coming over."

By now the sky had turned a dark, dingy gray. A color you'd expect to see in the dead of winter. But it was August now, and even in the northern states we were already feeling the unrelenting discomfort of summer heat. It must have been in the high 90s. Wade's light-colored shirt had dark stains forming under his arms.

I opened a bottle and prepared a rag that I had found in the warehouse. When Wade tapped on the side door, I quickly slid it open, grabbed him by his arm, and pulled him in. When we fell back onto my mattress, I wrapped my legs around his chest and pressed the chloroform-soaked rag tightly over his mouth and nose. He struggled and kicked a few times, but I used my free arm to secure a tight chokehold around his neck, which put him out even faster. Twenty seconds in he was as limp as a noodle.

I used the thirty feet of rope from the warehouse I brought to secure his legs together, and his arms behind his back. I placed duct tape over his mouth. In no time I had him wrapped up in a nice little package before he came to. And when he did, the panic in his eyes gave me an instant rise.

"Not what you were expecting?" I said, with a grin on my face.

Hours later the skies opened up and rain beat down upon the van roof. It sounded like pellets hitting a metal wall. The entire van was enshrouded with it, obscuring my view of the road in front of the lot. There were no signs of headlights. Nighttime had fallen and workers had already dispersed to their homes. I felt secluded in my mobile lair with my prey all tied up to my liking.

I lit a candle before I began my ritual.

I showed Wade the video of my legs tight around Randy's neck back in the warehouse as I squeezed out his confession. Wade tried to respond, but I hadn't removed the tape yet. I didn't want him to speak. What could he say to change my mind? The evidence was right there, clear as day. So I chose to keep his mouth bound shut.

I removed all my clothes and slipped on my black compression shorts. I played with my hard cock a few times, snapping it back to my stomach and stroking it a bit while Wade looked on. Then I poured myself some expensive vodka from the liquor store back home and sipped it while examining my latest capture.

Killing is a precious thing. It needs to be enjoyed. It needs to be savored. No rush job here, I'd come so far. I was proud of myself for having cracked this case. Maybe some ribs would crack in response. I had to think about this one. Take my time.

Wade tried to undulate a bit to free himself from the constraining ropes, but my knots were too tight.

I sat in the driver's chair, swiveled around to the back of the van, to enjoy his struggles. I was like a spider, and he was trapped in my web. Soon I would inject my legs and feast on his body.

A few hours in, I covered Wade's nostrils with my hands several times till he almost passed out. Then I circled his neck with several loops of extra rope and held it tight. His face turned cherry red and his cheeks puffed up. It aroused me more and more. And the rain kept coming down harder, which made the feeling even more intense.

By midnight, I was ripe and ready.

"Wade, I'm gonna have to kill you now, but before I do, I'll need you finger to unlock your phone." Wade panicked again. "Relax, I'm not going to cut it off." I turned Wade onto his stomach and held him down with my knee. Then I straddled him from top and sat on the small of his back. I swiped his index finger over the front of his phone until the cover screen disappeared. Wade groaned under my weight.

"This is how this ends, Wade. I'm typing to your buddies at Star Entertainment right now. *'Deal is off. We've been discovered. Don't think I'll survive this.'* That's what I'm sending." Wade grimaced when I pulled his head back and showed him the screen. "And…send."

I tossed his phone to the floor and slipped my arms around his neck. Then I rolled him over like a crocodile does once it latches its jaws onto its prey. I was now under his body, and my legs instantly crossed around his abdomen. I arched up and pressed my solid cock into his back. Then I slowly repeated that motion, tightening my legs and arms with each descent. My undulations were like the ripples of a snake's underbelly as it crawls along the jungle floor. If only I had more legs and arms, I would have surrounded him from head to toe. Not a single part of his body would escape my constriction.

"You'll want to enjoy this," I whispered in his ear. Then I figure-foured my legs and cinched them in. Once the first lower rib popped, I ripped the tape from Wade's mouth so he could scream out in agony.

"Go ahead. Scream all you want. It just arouses me more." On that, I tightened my legs again, and another rib broke free. "Two, if you're counting."

Wade yelled out, "Please stop!"

"I don't think you have much of a say in this, Wade." I tightened more, and he began to wheeze. "Save your breath. Just think of that mother and child that couldn't breathe and died in that house fire you caused. This is payback for them."

I tightened more and flexed my hamstrings in hard. I felt his internal organs begin to collapse together.

"I want this to be painful for you. I want you to suffer. So I'm gonna take my time."

For the next four hours I tortured Wade the developer with my legs. I used my arms to choke him out a few times, and when he awoke, it was full-on constriction again. In the process I came inside my compression shorts several times. His back was wet with my spunk and sweat. And when I was done, I pushed his lifeless body to the side and sat up on the side of the bed.

I downed a bit more vodka before driving my van onto the plot across the street, being careful to stay on the hard gravel area. I didn't want to leave tire prints. Then I opened the back of the van and dragged Wade's corpse into a deep trench that was already dug out for part of the foundation. I buried him a few feet under, just enough so his body would not rise up with the ensuing rain.

By the time I left the area and found a spot off the highway to park my van for the night, the rain had ceased. I fell asleep to the peaceful sounds of crickets outside my open window. It was as if the night had never happened.

Chapter 13

Morning sun sent golden shafts of light through the blinds of my side window, and I awoke to the smell of dried cum and stale sweat. Less than six hours ago I had killed another man inside my metal capsule. It had been a while, not since the dude down in the Louisiana swamps. I jerked off while looking at the remaining rope on the floor, the loops I used to choke old Wade. My desire to kill was satiated, for now.

As I passed by the development area, where Wade would forever rest, I witnessed cement trucks pouring wet concrete onto the foundation in the spot where I had buried his body. I smiled. How perfect an end to this particular case. I destroyed Wade's phone before I dragged him out of my van. No traces left behind. Now I had to figure out what to do with Randy back at the warehouse.

I arrived in Detroit just after 3 p.m. Franco was sitting in the same chair from two nights ago when I scissored his neck. A new, half-empty bottle of whiskey rested beside him. He had his legs propped up on my chair and his head tilted down. He was passed out.

"Franco." I put my hand on his shoulder. "Wake up."

Franco slowly lifted his head and greeted me with a half-cocked smile. "Hey man, you're back."

"Yes, I am. What's going on with Randy? Have you been keeping a good watch on him?"

"Yeah, about that." Franco reached for the bottle and took a long swig. "He's dead."

"What do you mean he's dead?" I snatched the whiskey from Franco's hand.

"I went in there and did what you did. I wrapped my legs around his neck and told him to give me a cut of that $20,000. You should have seen his face when he passed out. Fucking totally helpless. Then he never came to."

"Get up!" I pulled Franco up from the chair by one arm and the chair fell to its side. I walked him over and opened the door to the warehouse room. Randy was on the edge of the mattress face down. I checked his pulse, then rolled him over. His face was a pale white, but his lips were blue.

In a way, I was proud of my protégé boy. He learned to get what he wants using his body. But he also deprived me of what I desire, and need. I would have wanted to torture Randy more before turning him over to the police force. Now I had to think quickly on what to do.

"Franco. Help me carry him to his car. We'll put him in the front for now." We dragged the heavy man along under his arms. When we got the car door open, it took both our strengths to lift him into the driver's seat.

"There. That's good for now. Now for you. Follow me."

I led Franco to the small room. I told him to move the mattress to the side. Then I placed one of the folding chairs in the middle.

"Now sit in this chair. And don't move. And take off your shirt."

I left the room for a minute and returned with rope and one of my white T-shirts. I tied Franco's hands behind his back and his ankles to the chair legs. Then I tore the shirt into a long strip and rolled it up.

"Lift your head."

"Man, I'm sorry man! I didn't mean to kill him. Please don't killll me." Franco's speech was slurring from the alcohol.

"I'm not going to kill you. I'm just going to punish you. Open your mouth."

Franco tried to speak again, and as he did, I quickly pulled the rolled shirt across his open mouth and tied a tight knot with it behind his head.

"There, I've got you gagged. Stop talking."

Next I brought my chair in and sat behind Franco. I pulled out the electric clippers I had retrieved from the van and began shaving off his curly hair.

"Gonna change you, boy. Gonna make you the way I want you. Tilt your head down."

An hour later Franco's head was shaved close on the sides and barely much on top. I was transforming him into my boy. I wanted him to live and breathe by my every word. There could be no more mess-ups, like killing the cop. He needed to take my direction at all times, and always obey my commands. He would eat when I told him to, drink when I told him to, and piss when I told him to. He would be my creation.

Large beads of sweat formed on Franco's face as he burned off the alcohol. I wiped it down with a cool rag. Then I wrapped my big arms tight around his chest from behind and put my mouth close to his ear.

"You're mine, Franco. From now on, you work for me. You will be my fetch boy. I will send you out to mingle among the lowlifes and find me prey. Could be drug dealers, could be white-collar criminals. Could be just some thug asshole. You see, my appetite to kill grows stronger every day. You've witnessed the look in my eyes when my legs are squeezing the life out of someone. It arouses me, both mentally and physically. It's addicting, and you will be the one that feeds my addiction."

Franco nodded and rolled his head side to side as if he was about to begin a rebirth. My words were sinking in, and he could not escape me. I loosened my arms and stood up in front of him. I pressed the bulge in my shorts against his face and held his head there with my hand. I made him breathe my cock through the nylon fabric of my compression shorts, which was all I was wearing now.

"This is your future, Franco. I want you addicted to this smell. I never wash these shorts, because I like the smell of panic and cum." Franco started to pass out with my bulge tight over his nostrils. "Just breathe, boy. Breathe it all in."

After setting up my phone camera to record Franco's transformation, I left the room and locked the door. I told him I would let him out the next day. Maybe.

Later that night I headed back to the gym to get in a good workout. I needed to figure out my next move. The cop's body would smell in a few days, especially in this heat. And we couldn't stay in the warehouse forever. I pumped my leg and arm muscles extra hard while thinking things over.

Afterward, I popped over to the dojo to give Doug his private workout. He was telling me a new guy had joined the team. Big guy with big arms. Had knocked out our top submission wrestlers with chokeholds in record time. Almost crushed the trachea of one of the smaller guys, of which he quickly apologized. Doug showed me some video. Guy was pumped. Big pecs, smooth chest, solid biceps, and thick thighs. He'd give me a run, for sure. Name was Adrian. I told Doug I'd be back later in the week. Then I worked him with my legs one more time till he shot a second load. It felt good to be home.

I returned to the warehouse after picking up a large sub. I wanted to check on Franco before I slept. As I opened the door to the warehouse room, moonlight from a window across the way illuminated my hot shirtless boy in a blue hue. He looked great, all tied up and gagged. His head rested on its side and he was fast asleep. I woke him up by pressing my bulge into his face again. When he came to, I removed the gag and pulled off my trunks. I gave him a shot of whiskey, which he quickly swallowed. Then I placed my hard cock into his mouth all the way to my ballsack. His eyes looked up from the chair into mine as he pumped his mouth up and down my rod. Then I forced his head against it with my hand behind his head until I shot my entire load down his throat. It was an intense orgasm.

"My DNA is now a part of you, boy," I said, as I continued to hold him there tight. "It's your nourishment. I will nourish you often. And I will take care of you."

After giving Franco another whiskey shot, I fed him small bites of his favorite Italian sub. I kept his arms and legs bound to the chair the entire time. I liked looking at him that way. He didn't seem to care. He took in the food like a sacrament, for I was now his God.

"Tomorrow, we will take care of the cop," I said. "I have a plan. And we will leave here and start our lives together."

Chapter 14

Tiny sparks rose high into the air like fireflies seeking the warehouse roof. The popping sounds of heated metal echoed within the giant space. And the blast that followed shook everything inside. It didn't take long for the cop car to go up in flames, with Randy in the driver's seat and his phone by his side.

I had lightly dosed Randy's clothes with a can of gasoline we found in the corner. This was after I extracted the audio of Randy's confession that I had vise-gripped out of him and sent it to the media. Once I lit the match, Franco and I got in the van and sailed on out of there. We heard the inside explosion a few blocks away. It was a fitting end to the crimes: incineration.

Once again, we left no traces. The rope, the sub wrappers, Franco's pile of hair, and even the mattress were all set ablaze. The news anchor would announce the suicide of a rogue cop. Wade would be MIA, and his body would never be recovered. It was all neat and tidy. And the house fires would cease.

Franco and I spent the next few days hanging out at the gym. I got him hooked on the leg machines, of course, and we worked his upper body more too. At night he'd sleep in my van with me. I'd hold him tight within my arms and legs after he fed on my cock and balls for at least an hour. This was now mandatory.

Three days later, we stopped in at the dojo after hours. Doug wanted me to have a go with Adrian alone. Franco came to watch.

Adrian showed up in a pair of gray sweatpants cut off at the knee with purple trunks underneath. His chest was bigger than mine, but our legs were virtually the same. You could tell he had a strong core just by looking at his back muscles down to his ass.

He was quiet and brooding at first—just shook my hand and nodded when we met—but we immediately connected when our bodies began to intertwine on the mats. Doug watched from behind his office glass, and Franco cheered me on from the side.

At first I locked my legs around Adrian with my back to the mat, bringing him crashing down to his side. I squeezed tightly, but it didn't take long for him to escape and switch it up on me. I felt the power of his thighs around my own ribcage as he figure-foured my torso and throttled his hamstrings against my sides over and over. Then he slipped his left arm around my neck and sank my Adam's apple into the bend of it. His right arm slithered over his left wrist and behind my head. It was as if the tentacles of a science fiction creature were working me. He sank the sleeper in tight, but loose enough so I wouldn't pass out.

I struggled a bit to make him feel like he had the upper edge, but when I attempted my counter move, I was stuck. Franco yelled, "Get 'em, Marcus!" but I could barely move. Adrian rolled me to the other side, facing away from the two onlookers, and pressed his right ankle under my balls. I heard him say, "yeah man" into my ear before he tightened the choke. I wanted to stay in it forever, to be honest. I admired his confidence, and the bulge in my trunks showed. But I tapped to preserve my dignity.

Round two and I had Adrian's neck wrapped tight in my triangle choke, and his face turned a brilliant red. His cheeks puffed up and bits of spit exited from the corners of his lips. He looked like the final stages of death that I've come to enjoy so well.

But that fucker held on. Didn't pass out. And just when I thought I had him, he somehow pried my thighs apart with his big arms and broke free. It was astounding. That had never happened before. Even Franco was shocked.

"You almost had him, Marcus! Do it again!"

Of course, I tried again, but Adrian quickly pushed my legs out of the way and I felt the power of his pythonic arms around my neck again. His large, muscled pecs pressed into my shoulder blades. And once again he rolled me to the side with his bare feet brushing over my cock and balls. It was clear we were connecting in more ways than one. He found my weak spot and was taking full advantage of it.

For the rest of the match it was an even give-and-take. Three times I made him tap, so I thought, or maybe he was just giving me those wins. It was a good workout, for sure. Doug disappeared from the office window when we ended. I figured he had worked himself off just by watching us and left.

"Good match, man," Adrian said as we shook hands.

"Damn right it was. Finally someone here to give me a challenge." I laughed.

"I just moved to the area. Staying at the motel around the corner, room 21. Hit me up if you want to practice again."

"I will. Me and my bo-y…Franco here will be around. I've taken him under my wing and setting him straight. Keeping him out of trouble, you know. Hey Franco," I yelled, "let's get going." Franco was working some practice moves on a wrestling dummy in the corner. Adrian and I chuckled a bit.

"See you later, man."

That night I couldn't stop thinking about that match. Here, I always prided myself on being the badass of the dojo, and now this stranger comes in and makes me think twice. I hated him for that, but at the same time, I couldn't wait to feel those savage pecs against my body again.

But right now, my legs needed to feed on an unwilling victim.

I got Franco in the mood to hunt down someone for me. Someone we could both enjoy succumbing within my lethal grip. I told him to slip into areas where gang members hang out, and to keep his ears open for something that might go down. Could be a drug deal, a shooting, anything. Then he'd report back to me, and I would devise a plan to lure the prey to where I wanted him. But Franco had to return to my van by midnight to suck me off. Master's orders.

I liked having a full-time boy that would do anything for me. My possession of him was growing stronger. And I liked using a little alcohol as a reward to addict him to me. Even if he found no one for me to devour, I could still surround Franco with my thighs and calves in bed at night and crack a rib if I wanted. Sometimes he'd beg for it just so he could enjoy the pleasure of my pain. I toyed with him to make him want it more and more, but I never hurt him. I just made him stop breathing now and then in my solid grip. I was his holy serpent—seducer and constrictor. I controlled his air and his blood flow.

Three days passed and nothing. Much of the crime had moved out of the area when the fires stopped. Members of the police force patrolled the streets more often, just in case. It was an embarrassment to them that one of their own was found to be the perpetrator.

This was not going to stop my killing spree. My passion for killing grew stronger every day, if that was even possible. I liked how it worked itself within my head. I liked the stalking, the luring, and the taking. I think I've had this desire since puberty, maybe even before. I used to dream of being a creature that lived in quicksand. When unsuspecting hikers walked by, I'd thrust out my limbs, wrap them up tight, and drag them under. In grade-school recess, I'd be the monster in the center of the domed monkey bars, and as other kids tried to climb to the top, I'd grab them by their ankles and pull them inside the metal jail. I got aroused at watching an octopus' tentacles surround men in movies and hold them tight. Or vines coming to life and wrapping around a man's neck and torso. I wanted to be that octopus, that plant, those creatures that held their prey and killed that way. It seemed like a slow, pleasurable way to take a life.

One of my early victims was a jogger inside a secluded hiking trail. I was about 15, already big for my age, and on my way to becoming the star wrestler in my high school. But wrestling wasn't enough.

Guy must have been in his mid-twenties. One of those typical jogger types: skinny, lanky, pale, wearing those ugly jogger shorts that part on the side. Like something you'd see in the '70s. I felt he was a bad representation of the ideal male physique, so I had to destroy him. It would be a Darwinian kill.

He had passed me at the entrance, and I knew a secret entryway to the path about a mile up. So I road my bike ahead along the sidewalk that paralleled the woods until I found the part in the woods that would get me access. From there I would ambush him.

Twenty minutes later he stops right by me to catch his breath. I jump out of the bushes, grab him by his ankles, and roll us off the trail. From there I surrounded his thin neck with my legs and pulled his arms behind his back. He tried to push off the ground with his feet, but I was like a giant anvil that held him down. I figure-foured that neck and was able to get it locked in real tight. I had nabbed him from behind so he couldn't get a good look at my face, but I could tell his was getting redder and redder. Then he started to snooze.

I didn't kill him. I just knocked him out. It was such a rush, the capture and all. And I knew then that I wanted more.

Before he came to, I was already back on my bike heading to practice.

Chapter 15

On Friday night, while Franco was out on patrol, I ventured over to Adrian's hotel room to see if he wanted to hang out. It had been four days since our match, and I needed to find out more about this guy. I brought a bottle of whiskey over. Truth serum.

He opened the door and the first thing I noticed was the stubble on his face. He greeted me with a smile. "Hey man, come to get your ass kicked again?"

"I might be up for that, or me kicking your ass." I handed him the bottle of whiskey. "Something to celebrate a good challenge."

"Nice. C'mon in."

The room smelled of musk and sweat. Clothes were strewn over the king-sized bed and on the floor. An empty styrofoam carton from take-out rested on the edge of one of the nightstands. I sat in the corner chair and looked around.

"So, you got any cups?"

"Yeah, let me get them." Adrian returned with a couple of plastic-covered cups from the bathroom.

"This is all I got."

"Works for me."

I opened the bottle of Jack Daniel's and filled the cups halfway. Adrian smiled. "Whiskey won't weaken me. It makes me fight with more passion."

"Oh yeah? We'll see."

"Cheers!" We clanked the cups together, if you can call the sound made by two plastic cups hitting each other a *clank*. Adrian downed the whole glass. I followed.

"Oh fuck, that's good. I needed that." Adrian sat on the edge of the bed.

"So, what's up?" I asked.

"Just getting settled in. Looking for jobs in the area. Nothing coming up, yet. I applied at some gyms."

"Oh yeah? You a lifter?"

"I did for a while, but that doesn't pay the bills. Was a trainer in St. Louis for a while."

"Oh yeah, no shit? I was down there last month."

"You train at the dojo?"

"Nah, I just beat the shit out of those little guys. Make them think they stand a chance. Good practice, though."

Adrian laughed. "So I guess you can see that I am not a little guy."

I smiled and poured myself another cup. "I'd say we are about even."

"I thought you were trying to kill me with them thighs of yours around my neck."

Adrian hit my weak spot and I didn't know what to say. I mean, I didn't have my normal killing instinct when I was working his neck. I didn't even like to see him suffer. I just felt that I had to show him what I was made of.

"Maybe you can get payback tonight," I finally said. "Oh shit, what time is it?"

"It's almost 11 p.m."

"Well, the dojo is closed now, so, I guess another time…"

I tossed my glass into the basket in the corner and stood up. "I gotta use your bathroom? Mind?"

"No, man, go ahead."

When I returned, Adrian had already removed his shirt and slipped on his purple trunks. "Right here, buddy, on the bed. Or are you afraid you'll lose again?"

"Bring it, fucker," I said. I was hoping he was open to some mattress mayhem.

I removed my shirt and shorts and had my black compression shorts ready. We were both barefoot. We separated the mattress from the frame and laid it on the floor. After I downed another shot of whiskey, I felt Adrian's arms encircling my neck. *Fuck*, I thought, *here we go again*.

Adrian pulled me to the floor and wrapped his legs around my torso, just like at the dojo. It was like it was instinctual for him to assume this position of dominance and control. No one could pry those arms away, and he knew it. And his legs were like iron anvils. I felt helpless. I struggled and managed to turn my body around to face him, but he just countered with a front sleeper and locked his legs tighter around my abs. It was excruciatingly tight. And he didn't let up with his arms a bit.

Face to face, inches away, he watched as my eyes glazed over. I could feel the buzz of the blood flow cut off from my head. When I began to wheeze a bit, he just smiled. Then he let loose for a second and deep-mouth kissed me—not out of passion, but to remove more oxygen from my lungs. I felt weak, and I liked it. I was so aroused by this I'm sure he could feel my boner. And he did. He cupped it with both feet and held it tight.

For the next hour we writhed around each other and I let him enjoy any way he could work me. At one time he had me in a camel clutch with his arms still sleepering my neck. A couple of times he resumed his attack position and held his big hands over my mouth and nose, just like I've done to my many victims. I began to feel what it was like to come close to death in this way. And I knew why many of my prey stopped struggling. It felt good to die in the grip of another man. Something about this guy was siphoning the killer out of me. He was becoming my Achilles Heel.

Just as I was about to be knocked out for a third time, we heard a scream in the neighboring room. It was that of a woman. She was begging for someone to "Stop!" Adrian and I broke apart to listen.

"It's coming from room 20," I said.

"Please stop, let me go, no!" was repeated several times. Adrian and I stood up and listened through the wall.

Then we heard a door slam and a woman crying on the balcony. She quickly made her way down the cement steps and into her car.

We opened our door and took a few steps out. The curtains were parted and we saw the man in the adjoining room enter his bathroom. Then we returned to Adrian's room.

"Who is that guy?" I asked.

"I don't know. Some douchebag in his 40s that arrived after I got my room. I've passed him a few times on the way up."

"Sounds like he was fucking raping her."

"What do you want to do about it?" Adrian looked at me in an odd way when he asked that question. Like he knew what I *wanted* to do, and what I was *going* to do. It was as if he could read my mind. He was already master of my body.

"We'll wait till he's asleep and take him."

Franco gave me a call and met me at Adrian's room. I told him about what we had heard. Adrian was on board with us giving the guy a good work-over. But he didn't know my full intentions, *our* full intentions. How could I hide this from him? That I needed to feed on this guy? That I wanted to kill this perpetrator?

"You stay here, Adrian. Franco and I will check it out. We can handle this."

Franco and I left and returned to the van in the lot. I wanted to make sure Adrian was asleep before we made our move. Both the lights from his room and the neighbor's were out by 1 a.m. Franco somehow managed to copy the master key from the manager's office a while back when he was home-less. He told me he stayed in several of the rooms for free and no one ever caught him. My boy was turning out to be handy in many ways.

We both quietly returned to the second-floor balcony and made our way to the guy's room. The curtains were still parted, and we could see he was out cold on the bed. Franco opened the door with the master key copy, and we were inside feet away from the bed within a few seconds. I motioned to Franco to draw the curtains shut.

Mr. Raper man didn't come to until I was strad-dling his body on the bed in a schoolboy pin with my bulge inches from his mouth. I slapped his face a few times to surprise him with his demise. When he tried to sit up, I rolled him to the side and instantly crushed his lower ribs between my thighs. He spit up a little—probably the last swig of beer he had drank. The nightstand was littered with empty bottles.

"Hey fucker. You like to mess with women like that, do you? I got news for you, that ain't a way to treat a lady." I sunk my hamstrings in tighter as if they were thick jute rope cinching around a bale of hay. Air shot out of his lungs and he gasped.

Franco sat in the chair by the hotel heater and began rubbing his crotch.

"You getting this, Franco? You getting how nice it is to *kill* bad guys like this? Rub one out for me while I work him harder."

On that, I formed a figure-four with my legs around his abs and pulled on my ankle like tightening a drawstring. "No gaps, buddy. You are completely at the mercy of my leg coils." I thought about Diablo the giant python and how this guy was my pig prey. Flexing my feet, calves, and thighs as he exhaled assured that I was excising all his air. Without air, he could not yell for help.

Just then we heard a light tap on the door. Franco got up to check it out. It was Adrian. "Let me have his neck," he said.

I nodded to Franco to let him in, and Adrian joined me on the bed.

Adrian maneuvered his body up and around mine and behind raper dude so he was in the perfect position to lock his arms around dude's neck. It's one thing to be inside those big arms, and another to witness their power from the outside. I was so aroused by this. Adrian smiled at me as he applied the hold and tightened in.

"Let's make him suffer really good...before we take him," he said.

Chapter 16

Mr. Raper was one hell of a hot snuff job, mostly because I got to share it with another man of my caliber. We worked him so hard that the top half of his body was 180 degrees off from his lower half by the time we were done. Two big men can apply a lot of rotational torque, and the spinal column can only take so much. The torturing before that was insane.

At one point both Adrian and I had our thighs wrapped around his torso at the same time. As we squeezed, Adrian leaned in and kissed me deep. Below us were the gasping sounds of a man having his chest and lungs crushed. We fed off that sound as we embraced each other and stroked our cocks together. The harder we got, the quieter our victim became, until he was dead. At that precise point, Adrian shot his load onto my chest the same time as I did onto his. It was the best killer orgasm I could ask for.

Franco soon joined us, after we pushed the dead guy onto the floor. We had him suck both of us off in between strangling him nicely with our arms and legs. We both shot a second load and wiped it all over Franco's olive skin along with his own cum.

Franco was now bathing within the scents of two virile men.

After cleaning up, Franco and I rolled the body into a blanket and placed it into my van. We would later bury it next to an abandoned house far away from the city.

Adrian confessed that he had witnessed my alleyway kill in St. Louis. Ever since then he wanted to be a part of it. He followed me on my subsequent trips until he found the perfect opportunity to meet me on my home turf. He wanted his body to be a weapon for justice as well.

The idea of having a killing partner excited me. And with Franco on our side to sniff out more crime, we were unstoppable. Soon, we would form our own underground network of men that enjoyed using our techniques. Like a Fight Club, or Squeeze Club, as we called it. There would be a lot of bodies to hide.

I've never felt bad about my vigilantism, nor the ways in which I choose to kill my victims. Someone's gotta take out the bad guys. Even if an innocent hiker, or two, gets caught up in my neverending thirst for the scissor death grip.

More Books

Growing Up Wrestling
Men from around the world share their most personal wrestling memories from childhood to adulthood—a deep and intimate look at the homoerotic nature of wrestling and its cult-like grip on men of all ages. From being turned on watching pro wrestling on TV as a kid and not knowing why, to sneaking peeks at the amateur wrestling books to see the holds, these 130 stories reveal the universal attraction of wrestling for many men, regardless of sexuality. Guys candidly share their personal wrestling experiences with friends, cousins, uncles, classmates, bullies, and more. Order on Amazon.com

Growing Up Wrestling 2
More men from around the world share their most personal wrestling memories from childhood to adulthood—a deep and intimate look at the homoerotic nature of wrestling and its cult-like grip on men of all ages. A follow-up to the first book, Growing Up Wrestling. Order on Amazon.com

Visit WrestleMen.com for videos and more!